ANDY BRIGGS
VILL@IN.NET

Collision
Course

OXFORD
UNIVERSITY PRESS

To Dad, thanks for everything

OXFORD
UNIVERSITY PRESS

Great Clarendon Street, Oxford OX2 6DP
Oxford University Press is a department of the University of Oxford.
It furthers the University's objective of excellence in research, scholarship,
and education by publishing worldwide in

Oxford   New York

Auckland   Cape Town   Dar es Salaam   Hong Kong   Karachi
Kuala Lumpur   Madrid   Melbourne   Mexico City   Nairobi
New Delhi   Shanghai   Taipei   Toronto

With offices in

Argentina   Austria   Brazil   Chile   Czech Republic   France   Greece
Guatemala   Hungary   Italy   Japan   Poland   Portugal   Singapore
South Korea   Switzerland   Thailand   Turkey   Ukraine   Vietnam

Oxford is a registered trade mark of Oxford University Press
in the UK and in certain other countries

British Library Cataloguing in Publication Data

Data available

ISBN: 978-0-19-272968-2

1 3 5 7 9 10 8 6 4 2

Printed in Great Britain by CPI Cox &Wyman, Reading, Berkshire

Paper used in the production of this book is a natural,
recyclable product made from wood grown in sustainable forests.
The manufacturing process conforms to the environmental
regulations of the country of origin.

What a brilliant idea! One set of books,
featuring superheroes and one featuring
supervillains—and told through the eyes
of teenagers! Each series complete
in itself yet each referring to the other.
Original, imaginative and exciting!
Who could ask for anything more?
Excelsior!

Stan Lee

From: Andy Briggs
To: VILLAIN.NET readers everywhere
Subject: Careful on the web!

As you know, the Internet is a brilliant place to explore, but you need to be careful when using it.

In this awesome book, the villains (and heroes!) download their powers from the different websites. But VILLAIN.NET and HERO.COM don't really exist. :-(I invented them when I was dreaming about how exciting it would be to teleport into space. The idea for VILLAIN.NET suddenly came to me, especially the scene where Jake and Lorna have to fight the skeletons that come to life . . . But wait! You haven't read it yet so I'd better shut up! :-) Anyway, I began writing and before I knew it, the idea had spiralled into HERO.COM as well. But I had to make up all of the Internet stuff. None of it is really out there on the web.

Here are my tips for safe surfing on the web: keep your identity secret (like all good superheroes do), stick to safe websites, make sure a parent, teacher or guardian knows that you're online, don't bully anyone else — that's seriously not good - and if anyone sends you anything that makes you feel uncomfortable, don't reply, and tell an adult you trust.

I do have my own website, and it's totally safe (even without superpowers!): **www.whichsideareyouon.co.uk**

Be safe out there!

:-)

CONTENTS

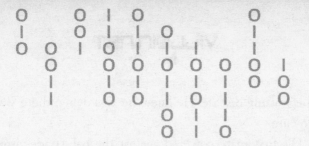

The Beginning

White-capped waves pounded the wooden-hulled galleon as it ploughed through the stormy sea. Lightning streaked across the sky, striking the mast and setting the sails afire. Even the heavy rain couldn't douse the flames as they consumed the Jolly Roger that crowned the mainmast.

The Buccaneer was a tough ship, but she couldn't take much more punishment. The damage was so heavy that she now resembled a ghost ship patrolling the high seas for unwary sailors.

Most of the crew cowered below decks, getting drenched with salt water as the sea flooded from above. Only three figures were brave, or stupid, enough to stay on deck.

The captain clung to the wheel, a rope around the waist binding him to it as he tried to steer the vessel headlong into the waves. If a wave broadsided the ship it would undoubtedly keel over, drowning all on board. He coughed violently, blood dripping from his lips. During the voyage he had developed

the wasting disease. He knew he was dying; there was no cure.

His first mate cowered against the balustrade, arms wrapped around the damp wood. A dozen waves had tried to dislodge him; only grim determination kept him anchored. The navigator had both arms and legs tightly wrapped around the mizzenmast, his eyes closed to battle the stomach-pummelling seasickness he felt.

The men were hardened sailors used to cheating the elements, but none thought they would make it out of this storm alive. They all suspected 1846 marked their final adventure.

'The storm is getting worse!' screamed the first mate. 'We'll die out here if we don't find shelter!'

'What will you have me do? I can't see or steer!' retorted the captain between hacking coughs. He had started to hate his first mate and the idiot's brother they had recruited as navigator. The brothers both possessed strange powers, a form of witchcraft that had driven them from their home town and made them take to a life of crime. The captain tolerated them because their unusual gifts were sometimes useful on raids.

'This is the devil's work!' cried the first mate. 'I swear if I get out alive I'll change my ways!'

'Use your gifts, man! Get us out of here!'

The Beginning

'There's nothing I can do!' snapped the first mate.

'What about your lousy brother? Can't he conjure up something? It's his fault he led us into this monsoon!'

'If he could he would! His ability is only—'

The first mate's words were swallowed as the boat was suddenly hoisted upwards on the crest of a wave with such ferocity that the force dropped both men to their knees.

The boat rose momentarily out of the sea as the wave dispersed beneath it—the vessel fell into the trough carved in the water. Timbers creaked, threatening to break.

'What in the name of all that is unholy . . . ?' muttered the captain as he suddenly realized why the wave had spectacularly broken. 'Look! LAND AHOY!'

The navigator ran to the railing and threw up over the edge. He wiped his mouth with his dirty damp sleeve as he stared thankfully at the land. 'At last we can get off this death trap!'

The wave had carried them into a sheltered bay. A dark island lay before them, lit for a fraction of a second by a bolt of lightning that revealed dense jungle and craggy rocks.

'We're saved!' cried the first mate, shaking his brother's shoulder. They both whooped and danced an improvised jig propelled by sheer joy.

The captain didn't join in. There was something about the jungle that felt wrong. He wordlessly guided the ship towards the pebbled beach.

Alerted by the change in the ship's movement, the crew had come out of hiding and watched with hope in their hearts as they dropped anchor.

The captain, first mate, and navigator headed ashore in a rowing boat, with four members of the crew, the only ones who had not weakened during the dismal voyage.

The navigator kissed the pebbly beach as the pirates landed. 'Oh! Beautiful land! It's so good to be back!'

The captain regarded the dark trees with suspicion. One of his men must have picked up the unusual vibe and stood with him, whispering.

'Don't feel right, Cap. Don't feel natural.'

The captain nodded. Then something caught his eye—a phosphorous purple glow amongst the trees. He glanced at the rest of the crew who were busy celebrating at the water's edge.

'Come on,' he nodded towards the jungle.

The two men used their sabres to cut away hanging creepers that blocked their path. The glow came from a boulder on the ground, no bigger than a man's head. They edged closer, finally seeing the source of the unusual light.

'It's a rock!' said the crewman in surprise.

The Beginning

The captain knelt, holding his hand over the stone. There was no warmth from it but the hairs on his arm stood upright as they passed through the electrically charged air. He didn't know what it was, but he sensed its importance.

He took a deep breath to cover the nerves he felt, then reached out and touched the stone. A spark jumped between the rock and his finger with a loud electrical crack. He jumped backwards; his crewmate already had his sword drawn, expecting an attack.

'Cap? Look!' There was no mistaking the tremor of fear in the voice. The pirate was staring at the captain's hand—

It was glowing! A fine luminescence clung to the captain's fingers as he flexed them. Strange sensations washed through his body.

'What is it?' hissed the crewman.

'I don't know. But whatever it is don't breathe a word to the others!'

To emphasize his point he wagged his finger at the man. A bolt of energy suddenly shot out and blasted a hole through the man's chest. He was hurled several metres backwards, hit a tree, and fell down dead.

The captain stared at his hand in amazement. How had he done that? He looked back at the purple rock. Whatever it was had given him the power, and he realized that the hacking cough, which had been tearing

his lungs apart, had disappeared. He took a deep, clear breath for the first time in weeks. The rock had given him power . . . and saved his life.

He crossed over to his dead companion.

'Rest your soul,' he said, running his hand across the man's eyes to close them.

At his touch, the dead sailor suddenly shot upright with a throaty gurgle. The captain recoiled in shock. The hole was still in the man's chest; big enough to put his head in.

In panic, the captain shot another energy bolt at his undead companion, killing him for the second time. The pirate collapsed and an eerie silence settled over the jungle once again.

The captain looked around. He would make this mysterious island his new home. An opportunity to make a difference.

A chance to put his mark on the world.

Shake Down

The earth shook with such a violent force that Jake Hunter was swept off his feet and crashed hard against the undulating pavement. He was groggy from the impact and fought to focus on the advancing lithe figure that bounced from the single-storey rooftops and landed in front of him. The moment the figure hit the ground, narrow fissures raced across the road and pavement in every direction.

One crack grew in size, swallowing an advancing car as it swerved out of the way of a toppling streetlight.

'Give me the pendant!' roared the villain. His voice was unusually high-pitched, perfectly suited for rising above the bass-heavy sound of the earthquake around them. His name was Seismic, and he was the epicentre of the devastation currently rippling across Los Angeles.

Cracks raced out in the concrete around Jake's feet, making a sound similar to breaking ice. Jake rolled as the road tilted sideways. The cracks deepened, creating a major fissure that formed in a complete loop around him. The slab of ground he was lying on suddenly dropped a metre as the quake raged. Water pipes cracked, spraying plumes of water high in the air around them.

'Nah, I don't think I will,' said Jake as he levitated so quickly that he head-butted Seismic on his way up. Jake grabbed the fiend by the scruff of his neck and elevated him several metres, offering an extensive view of the city as it shook all around them. From this vantage point, Jake caught sight of the motorcycle courier he had originally been chasing before Seismic showed up. The bike was making steady progress through the shaking city. He couldn't afford to lose it.

Seismic's beady eyes locked on to the pendant around Jake's neck. It was a white gem, held either side by a fine octagonal brass tube. Each of the eight sides was marked with tiny symbols. One end was raised in a series of bumps, the opposite end, a series of recesses as if others plugged into it like a building block. He reached for it—but Jake was too fast. He threw the man down so hard that he created an impact crater in the wide boulevard.

Jake suddenly fell to the street as his levitation wore off. He swore as he landed awkwardly. His powers had been sporadically glitching ever since the EMP, or electromagnetic pulse, had rippled through his body when he'd defeated Armageddon in Iraq. Something was changing inside him. Sometimes his powers would be stronger than ever, other times they would unexpectedly stop. It was annoying and making him nervous—what if his powers deserted him? He couldn't live as an ordinary boy any more, especially not now he was chasing the ultimate superpower separated into six pendants. It was a Core Power—the very origin of all superpowers.

He had already obtained three of them by duplicitous means. They had been held by prominent Primes—people born with powers—from both sides of the fence. They weren't around to claim them any more.

A higher authority had deemed that a Core Power was too mighty a burden for either a hero or a villain, and that made them all the more enticing.

The problem was that Jake was unaware of exactly what power he was chasing. In a way it didn't matter, as long as it was powerful enough to let him destroy both the Hero Foundation and the Council of Evil in retaliation for what they had done to him and his family.

The air shimmered centimetres from his head as Seismic unleashed a powerful shockwave into the asphalt. Jake rolled to one side and onto his feet, ready to counter Seismic's next move. That made him a target for any other Super wishing to possess the ultimate power. At the moment, only a handful of villains knew, but Jake was aware it was only a matter of time before

the Council of Evil discovered his treachery . . . and then things would really get interesting.

'What's the matter, Hunter? Lost your powers? Ah, I forgot—you're only a Downloader. Not a Prime like me,' gloated Seismic.

He probably thought it was the worst slur in the world, but Jake wasn't at all bothered. He responded by hurling a wall of force at Seismic. The invisible wall spun the villain across the street, throwing him into a hotel façade—the windows had already broken due to the quake.

'Looks like I haven't lost all of them,' chuckled Jake as he stood, catching his balance on the swaying ground. This was how most of his adventures had turned out—complete destruction.

He glanced down the boulevard and spotted his target rapidly disappearing. What the courier was transporting was of great interest to Jake.

The motorbike swerved through the cracks in the street and in between abandoned cars before ramping over crooked sections of crumbling road like a daredevil.

Jake would have flown after it, had his power of flight not disappeared earlier that day. He would have to rely on more traditional methods.

He raced across the street to retrieve his SkyByke— the cool gadget made for him by the Council of Evil's technicians. It had a complement of raw superpowers embedded into the electronic systems to give it an edge. Jake had last used it in Iraq but it had been badly damaged in the same EMP that had altered his powers. After that adventure, Jake had returned for the Byke, which street traders had already claimed and demanded money to return it. Jake had been in a good mood and had paid them, rather than fought them, so he could take it back to the Council's technicians, who repaired it. Now it handled better than ever.

He glanced back at Seismic, who had fallen to the ground, groaning from his injuries. Jake slid on his helmet and thumbed the fingerprint ignition pad to start the engine. It growled to life, audible even over the earthquake. The huge ball wheels powered through the debris strewn across the road as he gave chase. They allowed his Byke to move in any direction and over almost any terrain.

He had depleted the bike's flight power when he arrived in the city, so, until the machine was able to download another charge, he would have to proceed on the ground.

Jake weaved through the destruction: fallen telephone poles, power cables, building façades that had crumbled into the road, stationary traffic unable to move along the uneven cracked roads. The entire city was paralysed as the earth roared. He rapidly gained on

the courier who glanced in the mirror and throttled the engine to maximum overdrive, forcing the bike to pull a wheelie.

Jake's face was scrunched in concentration as he followed. The courier took some dangerous risks, made all the more precarious as the ground rolled like a wave beneath their wheels. No matter what stunt the courier pulled, Jake wasn't going to give up.

The courier turned onto another road and immediately the narrow motorbike shot between two stationary buses—cutting it so close both mirrors smashed off.

Jake's SkyByke was bulkier—there was no way he'd fit through and he was going too fast to veer around.

'Shields!' Jake commanded. The command activated the Byke's force field. The glowing shield hugged the machine and rider like a skin-tight suit, popping into place a second before Jake slammed through the narrow gap. The force-field absorbed the impact, forcing the buses' chassis to buckle as the Byke shot through. Passengers inside screamed even louder as their seats were bucked aside and the safety glass windows shattered across them.

The buses jerked apart as Jake bludgeoned through, his force-field disappearing the moment he was clear.

'That's it!' snarled Jake. 'Byke: plasma cannon!'

With a whirl of servomotors, a small cannon popped

Shake Down

from a recess above the front wheel. A head-up display (HUD) appeared on Jake's visor, tracking the movement of his pupil. He was so angry as he targeted the courier's rear wheel, that he momentarily forgot he didn't want to injure the rider.

'Fire!'

The SkyByke rocked as the cannon belched a dozen rounds. The courier had just that moment glanced behind and jerked the bike in a zigzag to avoid the volley. The plasma cannon tore chunks from the road, which took out several shop window displays, as the bikes shot along the trembling road at speeds approaching one hundred miles per hour.

The courier panicked and swung a hard left, rubber from the bike's wheels streaking across the intersection as the bike headed towards the hills.

Jake followed easily and tried to re-target the courier. A flashing red light in the top-right of his visor caught his attention. It was the threat detection. As soon as Jake glanced at it, the computer projected a small window showing the road behind him: Seismic was bounding in pursuit, each massive leap covering a hundred metres and sending tremors through the earth as he landed. The villain bounced from a building on one side of the street, careering like a rubber ball to the other side.

'Rats,' muttered Jake. That's all he needed. Ahead,

the courier zipped under a swaying bridge holding up the Hollywood Freeway. Jake could see all the vehicles' doors were open, abandoned as their owners had fled for firmer ground. He targeted the plasma cannon on the bridge.

'Fire—maximum power!'

Jake was momentarily blinded as the cannon pivoted upwards and shot at the bridge as he passed beneath it. Chunks of concrete bounced from his helmet as the distressed bridge started to collapse.

The SkyByke zoomed clear just as the freeway tumbled down on Seismic. Jake grinned with satisfaction as cars and trucks toppled over the gap the bridge had occupied and ploughed into the rubble below.

But his relief was dashed moments later as the rubble exploded and Seismic bounded out. Jake forced his gaze ahead as he roared through the narrow canyon, rubble trickling down the side of the hill, which he had to zigzag to avoid. This was compounded when the courier opened fire with a small machine gun. Bullet holes peppered the front of the SkyByke, fracturing the windscreen.

'Shields!' screamed Jake, but he had already used the small raw power charge aboard his bike. He had no protection from the bullets.

Behind, Seismic sent a powerful vibration into the side of the sloping canyon wall to Jake's right. Huge

Shake Down

boulders ripped from the hill and rolled towards Jake, leaving crushed scrub and palm trees in their wake. Jake violently swerved to avoid the larger rocks. The freeway ran to his left, but he couldn't take it as it was in gridlock with motorists who had slammed on their brakes the moment the quake had started. Besides, he couldn't afford to lose the courier. At least nothing else could go wrong.

Then his mobile phone rang. It was patched through to the hands-free kit nestled in the contours of his helmet.

'Hello?'

'Hi, Jake.'

Jake wanted to roll his eyes but he couldn't afford to take his eyes off the road. It was Lorna, his, for want of a better expression, girlfriend.

'What?' he asked irritably as bullets pinged from his Byke and a chunk of hillside slammed into his rear wheel almost causing him to lose his balance. He immediately regretted sounding so harsh, but this wasn't the best time to speak.

'I'm not disturbing you am I?' Lorna asked in a tone that suggested she didn't care if she was disturbing him.

'Um . . .'

'Only I'm having a really bad day and wanted some-body to talk to. The Foundation still won't give me back access to Hero.com and my brother is being a pain about the whole thing. What's that noise?'

'Um . . . just watching a film,' said Jake as the SkyByke bounced off a chunk of rock and soared several metres through the air before skidding back to earth.

Lorna had had her download privileges revoked by the Hero Foundation because they suspected she had assisted Jake in escaping from the Foundation hospital. Indeed, it was true, she had intentionally allowed Jake to leech her powers and flee after he had successfully, and this time, permanently, restored his family's memories.

Jake had a lot to thank her for, but whether he should still be *seeing* her was a question he couldn't answer.

He tried to sound calm and relaxed as bullets punctured fist-sized holes through the windscreen. 'Can we talk later—?'

'So I was wondering if we were still meeting tonight?'

Tonight? Jake had completely forgotten their arrangement and teleporting around the world through multiple time zones meant it was difficult to remember what day today was.

'Um . . .'

'You know . . . ' Lorna prompted, 'my birthday?'

Shake Down

Jake had completely forgotten.

'Um . . . I . . . er . . . '

A direct seismic shock hit his Byke, forcing it to accelerate forward, the tyres losing traction on the road. Jake had had enough.

'One second, Lorn.'

He pulled back on the handlebars, his increased strength allowing him to pull the wheelie on the heavy bike. He spun the Byke one hundred and eighty degrees—made possible by the Byke's unique spherical wheels. Keeping the front wheel airborne, he let the plasma cannon loose on Seismic.

'FIRE!'

'What?'

'Nothing . . . just a computer game . . . '

The plasma cannon covered the area around the villain in a curtain of fire. The dry scrub that formed the canyon walls ignited like tinder. Seismic tried to leap aside, but there was no escaping the violent onslaught—he was badly burnt and done for. His last act of survival was to teleport away before he succumbed to the flames. Jake saw the villain was hit and sent sprawling backwards into the thick black smoke.

'I thought you were watching TV?'

Jake expertly spun the bike back round and accelerated forwards—still keeping the front wheel in the air.

'I'm doing both,' shouted Jake as the Byke's front

wheel smashed into the courier, causing the rider to fall off the bike. The bike skidded across the road in a shower of sparks, bouncing off the safety fence that separated the canyon road from the freeway. The courier had somersaulted off the bike and landed in the softer scrub of the sloping canyon walls.

Jake ignored the rider and squealed to a stop at the stricken motorbike. The contents of the courier's pouch were of more interest. By the time he had taken several steps, the quake had subsided. He ripped the canvas back open and extracted a thin metal case.

'Don't move, Hunter.'

Jake slowly turned round. The courier was pointing a gun at him. The voice was female, which was confirmed moments later when she took off her helmet, revealing long raven-black hair and delicate Italian features.

'Who is that?' asked Lorna, a jealous edge in her voice.

'I'll call you back.' Jake disconnected the call and pulled off his helmet, it was sweltering underneath. Then he suddenly remembered he hadn't wished happy birthday to Lorna.

'Hand the case over or I'll shoot.'

'And if I do hand the case over?'

The girl smiled. 'Then I'll shoot anyway.'

Jake shook his head and laughed. 'Tough crowd.

Shake Down

Look, you have no idea what I'm capable of.' He stared at the gun, willing the atoms in the metal to heat up. They obliged and the gun glowed bright red in the girl's hand. She squealed and dropped it, sucking her fingers. 'See? I'm not what you'd call a normal boy.'

The girl looked at him with a curious smile. 'So I see. Then again, I'm not what you'd call an ordinary girl.'

Her fist suddenly shot out—extending several metres as her skin turned rubbery. Jake felt his jaw break from the unexpected punch. He fell back onto his bum, and felt the case swiped from under his arm before he landed. The girl stared at him with a lopsided grin.

'Oh, I know all about you, Jake.' There was a playful edge to her voice. Whatever she'd heard, she wasn't afraid of him. 'You're something of a legend at Forge.'

Jake had expected her to say the Hero Foundation. He hesitated. Forge was originally created by Mr Grimm, one of the few people Jake had ever fully trusted, and Momentum, a member of the Council of Evil. Their aim was to create a third super-entity that would act neutrally, and stop the dominance of either the Foundation or the Council. They siphoned super-powers from both Hero.com and Villain.net, and recruited Downloaders and Primes who were disillusioned by either of the main two sides. Grimm had trapped Jake, intending to use him as an ultimate super-weapon to destroy everybody else. Of course, it had all gone wrong, and Grimm and Momentum were now dead. The last he had heard, Pete Kendall, the kid he used to bully at school, now a renegade from the Foundation, was running Forge. Or at least, using their facilities.

'Legend, huh?' Jake couldn't help himself. She was quite cute. He pulled himself together; this was no time to be flirty and he had to remind himself that he already had a girlfriend. 'Then you know exactly what I've done . . . what I'm capable of?' The girl shrugged; a small gesture that irritated Jake. 'Give me the case.'

The girl wrapped her arms protectively around the case. 'No can do. These are documents revealing the location of an optical computer processor that Forge needs.'

'I think your glorious leader thinks he's more clever than he really is. What do you want it for?'

The girl smiled. 'I was going to ask you the same question.'

The answer was something Jake didn't want to give. He needed to find the quantum processor to help unravel the last part of his quest once he had all six pendants—there was a specific method of linking the pieces together, that required blind luck . . . or calculating a complex mathematical formula that had been put in place to confound anybody seeking the ultimate power. The key to the formula lay on the heavily encrypted Hero Foundation servers, known only to Eric Kirby himself, the leader of the Foundation. The optical processor would be able to break through security and retrieve the formula. If Pete wanted it, it meant Forge probably had the same goals.

He noticed that she was staring at the pendant around his neck with a hint of recognition. Jake felt stupid for wearing it. It was the first piece of the Core Power he had taken from a Council leader he'd had assassinated. The other two were safely stowed away on his person. Jake reasoned that if they were not all together, then nobody could get the full set of pendants if one was still hanging around his neck. However, it acted like a beacon to every other Super who realized the potential locked inside.

Jake pulled his shirt over to hide the pendant. The girl looked up quickly, aware that she had just been caught staring at it. She met his gaze levelly.

'So that's what you're looking for?' said Jake.

The girl shrugged again. 'Maybe. Look, I'm really sorry, but I have to go.'

'I don't think so.'

Jake lunged forward—but the girl simply vanished. Jake blinked in surprise. There was no telltale boom as if she had teleported, and he hadn't seen a quantum tunnel portal open up so where had she gone?

The fires lit by his plasma cannons had now consumed

the hillside, fed by the sharp Santa Ana wind that breathed through the canyon. The wildfire had caught up with Jake and the entire hill behind him was an inferno.

A giggling from behind made him spin round. The girl was standing behind him. He motioned towards her—but she vanished again. This time Jake caught the blur of motion and his head snapped round to see her stop behind him. She was using super-speed—and she was very good at it. Normally travelling so fast made moving in anything but a straight line almost impossible, yet she was able to circle around him.

'Too slow,' she taunted.

Jake spun round, his eyes narrowing. 'I'm not in the mood for games. Gimme the case, or I'll—'

With a loud whoosh the girl disappeared and a fast-moving breeze cut a corridor through the burning hillside, the flames extinguishing from the sudden movement.

The girl stopped at the top of the hill, half a kilometre away. Circled by flames, she waved the case tantalizingly. Jake could see that she was shouting, but the fierce crackle of the flames drowned her words.

'So that's how it's gonna be,' Jake muttered to himself. 'How about I fight fire . . . with fire . . .'

Shimmering blue tongues of flames suddenly leapt from his body. He could not feel the heat; in fact he could no longer feel the heat from the wildfire. Luckily the power didn't affect his clothing; at least his T-shirt and jeans didn't burn away. It would be too embarrassing to run after the girl naked.

On a good day, Jake could have summoned super-speed and given chase, but because of his erratic powers, he would have to resort to more traditional methods. He climbed aboard his SkyByke and gunned the engine. Luckily the machine was built to be fire resistant, so it functioned perfectly well even though he was blazing.

Jake revved the engine, and sped up the incline. The heavy orb wheels chewed through the uneven terrain without complaint.

The girl's smile slid from her face when she saw Jake closing in. She turned and ran.

Jake watched as the girl vanished, but the extinguished corridor amid the flames was a dead giveaway to the direction she was heading. The Byke easily peaked the hill, and Jake could see the girl's trail had already descended to the other side.

He gave chase, pondering if he should blast her with the plasma cannon. She was quick, faster than the Byke, but Jake could tell she was tiring. Super-speed was only really useful over short sprints; try to run a marathon with it and you'd soon drop from exhaustion.

Jake crested another ridge, this one offering a view across the hills, to the back of the Hollywood sign. The flames had not yet reached there, but they were threatening the canyon below him, which was dotted with houses built onto the hillside. They were all different, all unique—and all very expensive.

The flames had not yet made it over the hill, but when they did, the houses would be toast.

The girl suddenly became visible as she stumbled and rolled down the incline like a runaway car. Jake watched her smash through the front of one house, careering out the other side in a shower of splinters—before hurtling through the wall of another. The building absorbed her momentum and she didn't come out the other side.

'Gotcha!' yelled Jake.

He roared down the incline, smashing through garden fences and soaring over a swimming pool where a bunch of kids were playing water volleyball.

He skidded to a halt outside the damaged home and ran inside. The wooden walls, floor and ceiling suddenly ignited around him as he was still on fire, but Jake didn't realize, he was too focused on finding the girl.

A hole in the floor indicated she had bounced through the wall, and down to the entrance level—the layout of the house followed the steep hill it was built against.

Jake jumped through the hole—igniting another

room. Furniture burned as flames licked from his body. The girl was hunkered on the floor, clutching her shin, which lay at an odd angle. It was badly broken. If she hadn't possessed any healing superpowers when she fell, she would have surely been killed so a broken leg was nothing serious.

'Give me the case!' said Jake.

The girl looked at him in shock, tears in her eyes from the pain. She gathered her courage. 'You've set the house on fire!'

'I don't care! Give me—'

A section of burning ceiling suddenly crashed down, fanning the flames further. Jake sighed, he had had to rescue somebody from a burning building when he first manifested his powers and he didn't particularly want to do it again.

He quenched his flames, smoke rising from his body. 'Satisfied?'

'The room is still on fire,' the girl pointed out stubbornly.

'So is the rest of the hillside. Give me the case.'

The girl pressed the case against her chest, crossing her arms over it. 'I'm sorry, Jake, I really am. But I am under strict instructions not to let you have it. Forge wants to find the processors before you do.'

'Then I'll have to take it off you.' Jake took a menacing step forward. After everything he had been through with Chromosome and his own sister, he wasn't picky about hitting a girl. They often hit back far harder than boys.

'Under normal circumstances, I think we could have been friends, you know,' said the girl.

Jake hesitated. She was unusually calm. She smiled at him.

'My name is Orsina, by the way.'

Then she vanished with a boom. The rush of air that occupied the space where she had been was enough to extinguish the flames in the house. She had teleported out, case and all.

Jake kicked the wall angrily. Not only had she taken the one thing he wanted, but she had also been quite nice.

If the Professor wants the processor, he thought broodily, *then I need something to distract him. Jake didn't want anyone else interfering in his business, especially not Pete.*

The Professor was Jake's nickname for Pete Wilkinson, a kid Jake had bullied in school, who turned out to be downloading powers from Hero.com. Through an accident, Pete had formed the abilities to construct powers by unconsciously mixing the powers in his body. He had used those powers to poison Jake's parents, and that was something he wouldn't be forgetting in a hurry.

Shake Down

Jake had the ultimate revenge planned.

His mobile phone rang. With a sigh he pulled it out and glanced at the name on the screen: Lorna.

He sighed. It looked as if it would be a complicated day.

0
1
0
1
0
1
0
0
0
0
1
1
0
0
1
0
1
0
1
0
1
1
1
0
0
1
0
0
1
0
0
1
1
0
1

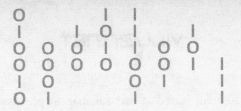

Complications

Arid Larkin was a weaselly man at the best of times. He had just risked his life in Toronto, stealing an advanced optical processor. The job had been simple. His contact was a teenage Italian girl who clearly had no business on the wrong side of the law, but she handled herself with assured calm. She had given him plans detailing the processor's secret location. Larkin had led his team of Special Forces operatives into the skyscraper to retrieve the chip from the vault. It had all gone to plan—until a bunch of kids arrived, flying and shooting the place up with powers he had never imagined existed.

By pure luck, Larkin had escaped and made it to the rendezvous point. It then turned out the girl was just a middleman, or rather, middlegirl, for the kingpin standing before him: his skin a sickly cyan colour, cracked and pitted. He had a wild, restless look about him. His frightening appearance was dampened by the fact he was only a young boy who went by the unthreatening name of Pete.

Pete Kendall stared at the transparent processor held within the impact resistant case. The light sparkled from thousands of tiny flakes suspended in the chip like glitter. It was a next-generation computer processor that could crunch massive amounts of data far quicker than any known supercomputer on the planet. This would help unlock the secret of the Core Power for Forge.

For several months, Pete had been running Forge since the Dark Hunter had killed its creators. The first months had been nothing but random raids because Pete and his associates had just wanted to have fun and vent their powers. But the ranks of Forge started to grow with Supers who had left both the Hero Foundation and the Council of Evil, and had seen Forge as a new beginning. This minority had started to shift Forge from a fun gang into a more serious player and Pete realized that if he didn't act to assuage the new members then he would have a mini-civil war on his hands, and they would no doubt turn against him.

Pete was saved from being overthrown by his reputation. Everybody knew that he had been one of the Foundation's rising stars and had fought Basilisk when he tried to destroy the Foundation. This had resulted in him being thrown through numerous vats of raw superpowers that fed the Hero.com website. Never before had somebody been exposed to such a mixing of volatile raw powers and the encounter placed Pete in a

Complications

coma. He was awoken by the Dark Hunter who had subliminally programmed him to attack the Foundation. Now Pete was a renegade from both sides, and imbued with the ability to combine the powers within his body into new ones just by thinking about weaving them together.

Both he and Jake Hunter had been called the 'Ultimate Weapon'. It was a great nickname, and made Pete feel powerful—a far cry from when Hunter used to bully him in the school playground. But then he heard about Core Powers and his attitude towards the Ultimate Weapon changed.

At first, Core Powers were mentioned as a whisper amongst older Primes, and regarded as nothing more than a legend amongst the younger generation. Pete had always loved a mystery, and searching for more information about them had reminded him of reading mystery books with his dad when he was younger. It was a favourite bedtime ritual they had. That triggered nostalgic memories of being at home with his parents before they decided to separate. Since his house had been destroyed and he fell into a coma, he hadn't seen them, and that made him feel abandoned and angry. He wondered where they were, but was sure that they hadn't noticed he was missing. These days, they were wrapped up in their own problems that didn't include Pete. Or so he thought.

That anger fuelled Pete's research. He discovered the Core Powers were the original root powers from which every other power had evolved. There were six in all, hidden across the world—perhaps, across the galaxy—that were deemed too powerful to wield. Pete had had direct contact with their destructive nature when he went up against Lord Eon, the master of time. But what the five other powers could be, he had no idea.

Every turn he took to search for the whereabouts of the Core Powers led to a dead-end. That was until reports surfaced that Jake Hunter was searching for them. These rumours were nothing substantial—the Foundation and the Council hadn't officially mentioned it. Then again, if they had, it would have confirmed such destructive powers existed.

The news created a ripple amongst Supers who believed the legends. Hunter was not only looking for them, but he had found parts of a particular one that had been hidden in the pendants. This had led to several Primes—heroes, villains, and Forge in-betweeners—trying to tackle Hunter to steal the segments off him. Pete was keen to fan the rumours just to get people to attack Hunter. Now Orsina had verified Jake possessed at least one of the pendants. That would just fan the rumours and speculation.

Pete was desperate to cling on to any new powers since he had discovered he had a shelf life. Either his

Complications

own gifts would one day abandon him . . . or he would die because of them. A Core Power could be his saving grace.

Larkin harrumphed, pulling Pete back to the situation at hand.

'Thanks, you did great,' said Pete.

'Yeah, but at a cost, right?' Larkin stared at Pete; he wasn't about to be threatened by a kid. 'I paid a lot of mercenaries for that job. I was the only one to walk out of there.'

'You knew the job was dangerous and you have been paid.'

'But I didn't know people would be flying around, shooting fire from their fingers, did I? I should get danger money for that.'

Pete sighed heavily. That was the problem dealing with crooks, they seldom stuck with the agreed deal and always asked for more.

'No,' said Pete flatly.

'No what?' asked Larkin with a frown. His hand was in his jacket pocket, his fingers touching the hilt of a gun hidden in there.

'No danger money.'

Larkin was angry. 'I don't think you understand what happened out there. It was a freak-show! Those people weren't normal!'

Pete's eyes narrowed, and for a moment they seemed

to flash with an internal light. Larkin was unnerved, and would have been further alarmed to know that Pete had just used X-ray vision to see through his jacket.

'Normal?' said Pete in a menacing low voice. 'Do you reckon you're normal?'

He lunged forward—his hand pressing against the concealed gun. He was so strong that Larkin felt the gun push into his ribs so hard he could no longer draw it out. Then he saw Pete's hand glow. The light was internal, so Larkin could fleetingly make out the bones, veins, and muscles beneath the red skin. Almost immediately he felt something incredibly hot against his chest. Pete pulled away. Larkin howled and threw his jacket off—the concealed pistol was now no more than a melted blob of metal stuck to his pocket.

'How'd you do that?' he screamed.

Pete snarled, he had no patience for bullies and extortionists. 'Apparently, I'm a freak. Now get out before something really nasty happens to you.'

Larkin spun on his heels and ran from the room. He didn't even pause to pick up his jacket, which contained his wallet.

Orsina peered over Pete's shoulder as he examined the chip. 'Now what?'

He wasn't sure. Pete crossed to a floor-to-ceiling panoramic window that offered a spectacular view from the mountain where the Forge base was located. It

Complications

looked out across the green forests and valleys of the Rocky Mountains. It was calming and allowed him to collect his thoughts. He didn't have enough information so the processor could unravel the complex codes that revealed how to use the power—but it was good enough that Jake didn't have it. Pete had the processor, Jake had some of the pendants containing the Core Power, and the Foundation possessed the key to unravelling the secrets.

'We wait. Hunter will come to us.'

'Are you sure that's a good idea?'

'When he does, we'll take the pendant from him. Then we'll have an element of the Core Power ourselves, and the key to use it. From what I've discovered, when all six pendants are locked together you have something unstoppable.'

'And when *we* get all six?'

Pete smiled. 'Then I think we'll be unstoppable.'

He suddenly grunted as a pain shot through him. A crushing pain descended on his chest. He dropped to his knees gasping for breath.

Orsina reached out to help him but a static-electricity spark bridged the gap from Pete's shoulder and her fingers with a loud crack. She yelped in pain and recoiled. More sparks crisscrossed Pete's body.

'What's happening to you?' said Orsina, sucking her fingers.

Pete's teeth clenched because of the pain. Then it suddenly stopped. He lay flat, panting for breath and dribbling on the hardwood floor. He felt sick. He knew what was happening to him, Jake had warned him many times. In revenge for trying to poison Jake's parents, the villain had planted an artificial virus within Pete. A virus that would slowly kill him. Jake had been using it to taunt and blackmail Pete, but now he had finally triggered it.

Pete knew his days were numbered.

Jake Hunter smiled as he leaned back in his chair, enjoying the cool breeze from the room's air conditioning. He had returned to his private island at the Council of Evil headquarters so he could activate the surprise viral bomb he had secretly implanted into Pete the last time they had met.

If Pete insisted on interfering with Jake's plans, then he had to pay the price.

Jake walked to the door that swished open before he reached it. He stepped out onto the walkway that connected his island to the central hub of the COE network. Each Council member had their own small island which circled the main island, which was populated by huge towers and domes where the COE staff worked, issuing permits to supervillains so they could

Complications

conduct their evil plans, creating global ransom demands, and making sure the Hero Foundation never got the upper hand. The main island was filled with thousands of clerks, ambassadors, and technicians who created the coolest gadgets and ensured Villain.net ran smoothly—which was no small task since it was pirated from Hero.com and had never worked properly from the beginning. The main island was a vast city in its own right.

Jake leaned against the walkway's handrail and looked down at the crashing sea. The air was tropically warm and seagulls cawed noisily overhead. The refreshing saltwater spray rejuvenated his tired eyes. He took a deep breath that helped him focus his thoughts. He pushed aside his guilt at launching a ticking bomb inside Pete.

Pete had created a poison and tricked Jake into using it on his parents to restore their memories of him. He had been coerced into doing it by Momentum, a Council member—a dead Council member, Jake corrected himself—but that didn't make Pete's deed any more palatable.

After all his adventures, Jake now felt closer to his parents, although he seldom saw them. It seemed that the Foundation had considered the truth about Jake to be too much for them to handle so had set up a cover story in which he had been placed in a special school

for delinquent children and their daughter had been isolated because Jake's behaviour was corrupting her too. He was sure some side effects of their amnesia had aided them in accepting the story, and his own track record helped enforce the lie. However, the cover story worked well for all parties concerned, so Jake didn't challenge it.

Now, the only wrinkle in his family was Beth who had been brainwashed by the Hero Foundation to kill him.

Jake glanced across to Momentum's island. It had remained empty since his death. In fact there were very few Council members left, thanks to Jake.

Momentum, Chromosome, Amy, Armageddon, and Professor Mobius—all deceased. That only left Fallout, Abyssal, and the unofficial leader of the Council, Necros. Necros was a tough villain, and possessed one of the pendants Jake needed. Getting that one worried Jake considerably.

His phone suddenly rang. He groaned when he saw Lorna's name on the display. Wouldn't she leave him alone for five minutes? He cancelled the call and turned off his phone. He had serious business to attend to.

High winds tore at the prayer flags mounted along the

Complications

narrow winding track that led up the steep mountain-side to the monastery. Jake stepped through a shimmering portal that split the air in two; behind was his warm chamber in the Council of Evil. As soon as his foot was out, the portal closed with a swishing noise.

Jake shivered as snow blasted against him, numbing one ear; a rapidly clacking prayer wheel deafened the other. He had been to Tibet on several occasions and had yet to quantum tunnel to the exact location. He didn't know if that was some kind of defence surrounding the monastery, or if his powers were not working properly. He made a mental note to get checked out by one of the Council's physicians.

He began the slow climb up the winding staircase to the high walls, etched with Buddhist carvings. It was a place of serenity and calm, and the home of an ex-superhero who wanted bitter revenge.

An orange-and-red-robed monk opened a smaller door built within the larger ones like a giant cat-flap. He knew Jake by sight, but refused to look him directly in the eye. The monk led Jake into a dark warm hall that was rich with the scent of exotic spices.

The monk motioned for Jake to sit before a huge fireplace that gushed waves of heat out so intensely he had to sit several metres away. Jake had no sooner sat down, than he noticed the monk had vanished without a sound. The way the monks disappeared and appeared without observation convinced Jake they possessed some type of superpowers.

'Ah . . . Jake, my boy,' echoed a frail voice across the hallway.

Jake followed the sound. An old man hobbled across through the shadows, walking with two canes. Jake made no move to help him: he had tried that once, and the old man had taken great offence. The man sat down opposite Jake, light falling on his wizened face for the first time. Jake gasped.

'Leech? What happened to you? You look . . . look . . . '

'The years are catching up on me fast, are they not?' He took Jake's silence as an agreement. 'I'm much older than I look. How about that? I age differently from normal folks. But . . . even age can be broken. It is a form of immortality, a power over life and death.' He stared thoughtfully into the fire, then suddenly changed the conversation. 'So, what news do you have?'

'The optical processor you said we needed . . . I couldn't get it. Forge has it.'

Leech looked disappointed. He stared at the flames. 'You still have your three pieces of the pendant safe?'

Jake automatically touched the one hanging beneath his shirt, then regretted giving away its location to Leech. He hoped the old man hadn't noticed, and he

Complications

gave no indication that he had. Jake didn't trust him. After being betrayed by Mr Grimm, Basilisk, and his own sister, who had been brainwashed by the Foundation, Jake didn't trust anybody. He had already made the mistake of telling Leech he possessed half the pendants.

'They're safe. I know Necros and Kirby have one each, but I'm still no closer to finding the other piece.' Leech grimaced at Kirby's name. 'So what's the deal with you and Kirby? Why do you want him dead? Is it because of what he did to your son?'

Armageddon was a member of the Council of Evil who Jake had disposed of. It turned out Armageddon was Leech's son—taken from him at a young age by Eric Kirby, the leader of the Hero Foundation. When Jake had revealed he had half the pendants, it had meant telling Leech that his son had died. The old man betrayed no emotion, and Jake didn't think he should mention he was the one responsible for disposing of Armageddon.

Then again, maybe Leech already knew? He had a peculiar second sight power that allowed him to see events around the world. It was a power Leech had sucked from Eric Kirby, and because of this, Kirby had banished him to the remote temple. Branded an outcast, never to set foot in the civilized world again. This had made Leech bitter and resentful.

Leech drummed his fingers on the chair, his gaze firmly fixed on the fire.

'You know I once possessed this Core Power you seek?'

'So you said. Why won't you tell me what it is?'

'Because you need patience to wield such power, and anticipation does little to help patience.'

'You're talking in riddles again. I don't mind telling you that I'm getting a little fed up. How do I know you're not making me run around in circles? This could all be complete rubbish.'

'How many times have you been attacked for that pendant around your neck?' Jake looked sheepish, maybe there were no secrets he could keep from Leech. 'Others know of its power. And if you wanted to use it . . . you could.'

'What? Now? Without all six pieces?'

'Only with all six parts will you have the full power. Each pendant is a fraction of the whole. With each part the power grows exponentially—in other words, it becomes more and more powerful. Combine the three you have together, you can tap into the smallest reaches of the power but it would be barely noticeable. But with the addition of a fourth . . . then everything changes. The power strengthens with each piece. Remember, the Core Powers were placed beyond use for a reason! Unleash their destructive power now . . . and you'll be unstoppable!'

Complications

'So why bother searching for the other pieces?'

'Because what you have now is not enough. When I possessed the power . . . I realized I could control not just the world . . . but entire galaxies!'

Jake felt uneasy at the hint of madness in Leech's voice. He'd heard that tone many times in other megalomaniacs.

'So, Kirby split you and your son up. You worked for the Hero Foundation, your son became a member of the Council of Evil; you leeched one of Kirby's own powers after he stripped you of the Core Power . . . and now you want revenge? Right? Have I missed anything out?'

'It's a simple plan.'

Jake didn't reply. Nothing was ever so straightforward. 'I know what powers Kirby has. But what about Necros? Nobody seems to know what powers he possesses.'

Leech smiled enigmatically. 'Necros is an old pirate. A keeper of secrets.'

'That really doesn't help me.'

'There are some answers you want to know and others you need to know.'

Leech held up his hand. An ornate chest that was lying in the darkness suddenly scraped along the stone flags, pulled by a telekinetic force. It stopped under his hand. Jake had seen the chest the first time he had met Leech.

'Perhaps this will answer your question.' The lid creaked open, and Jake could see a number of bound scrolls and books packed tightly inside, amongst some archaic looking electronic equipment. Another casket inside emitted a purple light. Leech extracted a photograph and snapped the lid shut.

He handed the picture to Jake. Two men were shaking hands. Behind them lay huge empty glass vats that would one day contained raw superpowers. Jake immediately recognized Eric Kirby. It took a few moments before he realized the other man was Leech. Jake glanced at the back of the photo. A faint pencil marking read: 'The Kirby Boys'.

'You're related?'

'Eric is my brother.' Jake was astonished. After everything that had happened to his own family, he knew the pain Leech felt. 'This was the day we finished construction of the Foundation headquarters. The one Basilisk drove into the Mongolian desert. It was a great technical achievement that predated Hero.com. The idea was to synthesize superpowers, using my leeching skills to extract them from Primes so they could be duplicated and placed in those vats.

'As you know, most Primes naturally possess just a couple of powers. Most were jealous of the idea that a normal person could experience more powers than they could. The original scheme was to recruit people

Complications

from newspaper adverts. We placed small ads in the classified section, and then later bigger advertisements in the backs of comic books. Back then, in a comic book, you could buy X-ray glasses, instant muscle kits, hypnosis sets . . . everybody thought they were toys. In actual fact, they were devices that contained raw superpowers. Those people were our original Downloaders. The advent of the Internet made it easier to distribute powers . . . and you are familiar with the story of how the Council pirated Hero.com to create Villain.net. I think Kirby never wanted me to be part of the Foundation. He envied my ability to sample other people's powers. That's why he made me an outcast.'

'So you want me to bring down the Foundation?'

'No. I believe you want to do that. I want you to kill Eric Kirby.'

'I'm not an assassin!'

'You killed my son!' spat Leech, a snarl disfiguring his face.

Jake had no comeback to that. He didn't think it was the time to point out that Armageddon had triggered a nuclear bomb to kill himself. The electromagnetic pulse that the explosion generated was the same one that was playing havoc with Jake's powers.

'Kill Kirby, and you shall have his piece of the pendant. Then, and only then, will I tell you how to defeat the most fearsome Prime of them all, Necros—you should leave his piece to last. With my help, you will have severed the heads of both organizations and will be the sole owner of the Core Power I once had!'

The echoes of Leech's tirade faded and silence once again filled the hall. Finally, Leech reached into the chest and pulled out a laptop-sized device that was as thick as a dictionary. It was made from yellowing plastic, which once must have been white, and had a single grey screen in the centre.

'But before you face Kirby, there is one more piece that is in easy reach. Take this.'

'It's a piece of junk.'

'It was made in the 1980s. It was state-of-the-art back then. This will lead you to an electronic marker that will reveal the resting place of the missing pendant.'

Jake thumbed the chunky power switch. Nothing happened. 'It's broken.'

Leech held up a plug. 'You have to plug it into the wall first. The pendants were distributed equally amongst the Foundation and Council. Over time, members of the Council killed their counterparts in the Foundation to retrieve all the pieces. One remained with a hero who vanished two decades ago. He was eventually found dead, but without the pendant. I have conducted years of research and through personal papers, I eventually found out he was on a sensitive mission. He left markers along his path, like breadcrumbs.

Complications

All we have to do is retrace his path and find the pendant.'

'How do you know he still had it when he died?'

'Because it never surfaced again. The Primes who killed him were hunting the pendant. To carry one makes you a target.'

Jake nodded. He knew that feeling. Carrying one was bad enough. When word got out that he had three . . . then he would be a real wanted man.

'I have detected one of his markers in a museum. That is where you must start searching. When you have the fourth piece, I will show you how to unlock the four pendants you have, because you will have to use their combined strength to defeat my brother. Let me see the one around your neck.'

'I thought that's why I needed the processor?'

Leech smiled. 'I know the permutations for four of the pendants. I have had some . . . previous experience with them after all. For all six, well, that's a mathematical problem I can't calculate without the key. Only Kirby knows that combination.'

Jake reluctantly pulled the pendant out. He kept a tight hold of the leather cord around it. Leech examined the gem held within the pendant with greedy eyes.

'Ah yes . . . exactly how I remember. The fragment power is held inside . . . ' He stroked a finger across the surface. Jake yanked the pendant from his hand. That brought Leech back to his senses. 'The lure of great power is attractive. Even to old men. As I have mentioned, I have had experience with this power before. Once you unleash such fury . . . it has a hold on you. Look at the ends of the pendant. Do you see the markings?'

Jake examined the pendant.

'The symbols must be aligned correctly to use the power to its full potential. To align them incorrectly is disastrous. Just one piece can connect to a specific end of that pendant. So you have a one-in-six chance of connecting the right one. Then, you have to ensure the octagon faces are in the correct order. The odds of getting all of them aligned correctly are very high. Astronomically high in fact once the permutations are factored in. It's more difficult than winning the lottery!'

'So that's why I need the processor Forge has?'

'Alas, yes. But we'll cross that bridge when we come to it. For now, follow the trail and be careful. If I found this out, others will have done. There are many Primes who have been searching for a piece of the ultimate prize. They will use everything at their disposal to beat you to it.'

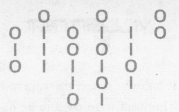

The Hunt

The enclosed courtyard leading up to the doors of the British Museum pooled with rain puddles as a tempest rumbled above. Jagged lightning licked the sky, the thunder amplified by the concrete canyons of the surrounding city.

Jake eyed the Greek-temple-styled building suspiciously. He hated museums. His very first memory as a child was being lost inside one as it was closing up for the night. At five years old, there is nothing more terrifying.

He leapt effortlessly over the cast iron railings surrounding the courtyard. The building had been shut for the last six hours, so the only signs of life inside would be the security guards. Before leaving the Council, Jake had browsed through Villain.net to replenish his missing powers. He was glad to have flight back, but knew it could expire at any moment. He had also located a power that rendered him invisible to security cameras, laser tripwires, and heat sensors, so he wasn't worried about triggering any alarms.

He made it halfway across the courtyard before his phone rang. The Ironfist guitar solo he had chosen for his ringtone echoed across the yard with its high-pitched chords. He scrambled to answer it.

'What?' he hissed in a low voice.

'Jake! It's Lorn.'

Jake immediately felt uncomfortable. He had apologized for missing her birthday, and to her credit, she hadn't asked why he'd missed it. But since that call he had been dodging Lorna's phone calls for two days. She was still grounded from Hero.com and used all her free time trying to see Jake. They were supposed to be dating after all.

'This isn't a good—'

'Where have you been? I've been trying to get hold of you for ages.'

'I'm on a . . . mission.' Lorna was fully aware of Jake's villainous status, although she refused to accept he could be so bad.

'Cool. I'll come and join you!'

'No, Lorn. That would be a bad—'

Jake was suddenly punched in the ear. He fell to the floor, dropping the phone as a black mass oozed from the display screen. He blinked in shock as the mass congealed to form Lorna. She was grinning, holding her own mobile. She hung up and retrieved Jake's phone, offering him a helping hand to stand.

The Hunt

5

'Sorry about that. It's a new power I found. It automatically traces your call. Cool, huh?'

Jake snatched up his phone and didn't return the smile. His ear was throbbing. It was an odd fact that he could take fireballs or laser blasts and the combination of his shields and super-healing would numb the pain, but a good old-fashioned punch to the ear hurt like crazy.

'Lorna, I'm right in the middle of something!'

The smile never left her face. 'I'll help.'

'Believe me, this isn't something you want to get involved in.'

'Well, since the Hero Foundation barred me from having any fun, I can make up my own mind about what I would or wouldn't like to be involved in.'

'Well I . . . hold on, how did you get here if you're not using Hero.com?'

Lorna waggled her mobile. 'I stole my brother's phone. I'm using his access.'

Jake felt a glimmer of respect for Lorna. She was showing some villainous attributes . . . was that a good thing? Jake shook the thought away; morals had no place here and he couldn't afford to risk precious time arguing with her.

'We've got to get inside here. I'm looking for something.'

'What?'

Jake shrugged. 'I have no idea.' He pulled the clunky tracking device Leech had given him from a backpack. 'But this will point the way.'

They approached the firmly locked doors and Jake mentally cycled through what power he would need to get through.

'Grab hold.' Lorna's fingers sank into his arm and he triggered his apport power that allowed him to travel over a short distance. The whole world flip-flapped as if made from rubber. The door vanished, replaced by the Great Court—a wide-open space with a white circular building in the centre and white Greek Revival architecture all around. Lightning flickered overhead, and rain pounded on the massive glass and steel roof, artfully constructed from one thousand six hundred and fifty-six triangular panes. Information kiosks, souvenir stands, and a silent café stood in the darkness. Several doors led into the exhibition spaces. It was a spectacular space, but Jake was too busy looking around for a plug.

'This is amazing.' Lorna's whisper echoed around the cavernous interior.

Jake found a power outlet with a warning sign claiming it was only to be used by cleaning staff. He pulled a long extension cable from his pack, and plugged it into the wall. The machine slowly switched on as the valve-powered screen warmed up with a creaking noise.

The Hunt

Finally the screen glowed green, a single blip pinging to the north-east. Jake slowly turned round until the blip was dead ahead. The signs declared it was in the Ancient Greece and Rome section.

'Got it . . .'

'Freeze!'

Jake groaned. He hadn't seen the security guard creep up on them, and Lorna was too busy marvelling at the expansive chamber to notice.

'Hands up!'

Jake raised his hands and slowly turned to face the plump security guard. He had a futuristic looking taser x26 stun gun in his trembling hand. His finger hovered over the trigger, ready to deliver three hundred kilovolts of electricity that could floor any would-be attacker.

Jake was puzzled. How had they detected him? He glanced around, noticing that a security camera discreetly hanging in the corner of the yard was pointing at Lorna. He groaned. While he was invisible to the cameras, Lorna wasn't. Her presence had triggered the alarm.

The security guard looked around for any visible sign of forced entry and seemed confused when he couldn't find any.

'How did you get in here? Were you hiding when we locked up? What's that in your hands?'

Jake glanced at the scanner held above his head, and,

before he could stop himself, the words blurted from his mouth. 'It's a bomb.' The guard went pale. 'And if you shock me with that thing . . . it might detonate.' Jake was proud of his improvisation.

The guard's radio crackled to life. 'Dan, I've got you on the monitors. What's the hold-up, over?'

'Don't answer,' warned Jake. 'Whoa!' He made a pretence of almost dropping the scanner and the guard jolted forward to catch it, before remembering to keep his distance.

'My partner will have already phoned the police. They'll be on their way right now.'

The radio crackled again. 'Dan, I don't know if you can hear me, but the phone lines are dead. They must've cut the wires!'

Security guard Dan rolled his eyes as his partner blew what little leverage he had over the intruders. Jake frowned.

'We didn't cut the wires.'

'Like I believe that.'

A feeling that something was wrong came over Jake. His eyes scanned the darkness.

'Listen . . . I know you won't feel like believing me, but something isn't right. Somebody else is here.'

The guard's eyes darted around the hall before fixing back on Jake. 'OK . . . put the . . . bomb . . . on the floor. Gently now.'

The Hunt

'Or what?'

Dan hesitated. It was a good question. Lightning flickered overhead, casting a network of shadows from the steel mesh roof. Amongst the shadows, Jake saw a silhouetted figure, spread-eagled and plunging towards the glass almost directly above him.

'There!'

The guard instinctively followed Jake's gaze—and regretted it. Jake vanished—and appeared directly behind the guard. Before the man could react and re-aim, a section of glass and steel crashed away overhead as the newcomer ploughed through.

Lorna screamed and dived under a souvenir stand for cover. Jake hauled Dan aside as a steel beam split the floor where he had been standing.

The intruder landed on his feet, absorbing the impact with a crouch. A massive pair of eagle wings protruded from his back, and his eyes glowed brightly in the gloom. Jake saw a Hero Foundation logo fastened to his chest.

'Hunter!' bellowed the stranger in a gravelly voice. 'I've come to punch your ticket. Time's up! Maelstrom is here, so gimme the pendant, and I might just let your traitorous girlfriend live.'

Jake didn't care who the rampaging hero was, his intentions were clear: he wasn't trying to stop the Dark Hunter for the good of the Foundation, he was out to

rule the world. Leech had warned him that the lure of the Core Power would bend the will of even the most valiant crusader.

Dan still had his taser outstretched. Jake gripped the guard's hands—his enhanced strength easily forcing the taser towards Maelstrom—and pushed Dan's fingers against the trigger—

The shot would have gone wide, if it hadn't been for the hero's wide eagle wingspan. The barbed darts easily punctured the thin wing, trailing a wire back to the taser. A fraction of a second later the powerful electrical charge gushed down the wire and into the hero.

The winged freak jerked as the voltage powered through his body, then he collapsed, temporarily paralysed, on the ground.

Jake pushed the shocked security guard away. 'Run! When he gets up, you don't want to be around!' The shocked guard couldn't tear his gaze away from the winged monster. Rain poured through the hole in the ceiling, drenching him. 'I said run!'

The guard suddenly came to his senses and fled from the room. Jake rushed over to Lorna and pulled her from under the stall.

'Let's go before he wakes up.'

'We're too late!' she wailed.

Jake glanced over his shoulder as Maelstrom rose on

The Hunt

one knee and glared at him. A stream of blue energy pulsed from his eyes and struck the souvenir stall. Wood and charred bric-a-brac cascaded over both Jake and Lorna.

'Follow me!' Jake led Lorna towards the 'Greece and Rome' doorway.

'Scum like you can't escape from Maelstrom!'

A torrent of blue energy cracked the ground at Jake's heels. He shoved Lorna through the door—before noticing the snaking power-lead from his scanner had wrapped around Maelstrom's feet. Jake yanked the cord tight. The cable tangled around the hero's legs as it snapped taut—he fell hard on his back, crushing his delicate wings with a howl of pain. The scanner's power lead popped from the extension cable allowing Jake to sprint through the doorway.

Jake ran for several metres before he stopped, swathed in gloomy darkness. He could just discern that the room was dark and long, lit only by red emergency lights above. It took a moment for Jake's eyes to adjust—and when they did he was nose-to-nose with a furious snarling jackal. He leapt backwards before realizing it was just a black obsidian statue—a jackal head on a human body.

'Anubis,' whispered Lorna close to Jake's ear—causing him to jump again. 'Why are you so twitchy?'

'I don't like museums.'

As his eyes adjusted further, he could make out rows of ancient Egyptian statues—gods, pharaohs, and needle-like monuments raised to the heavens. The select trophies of a long-dead civilization.

Maelstrom's bellows echoed behind them . . . then silence as the thug undoubtedly realized he was giving away his position.

'That guy's supposed to be a hero,' whispered Lorna. 'Why is he so mad at us?'

'He wants the same thing I do.'

'And what is that?'

'I'll tell you when I find it.'

'After everything we've been through, you don't trust me enough to tell me what we're looking for or where it is?'

Jake looked around, confused. Running from the court into darkness had disoriented him and he couldn't visualize in which direction the scanner had been indicating. He needed to plug it in again.

'Look for a mains socket.'

'Huh?'

'I need to get this scanner working again.'

They crept across the polished floor, heading towards the nearest wall. There were no power sockets visible.

'There's got to be one . . . ' Jake trailed off as Lorna tapped his shoulder and pointed behind. He couldn't see anything, but he could hear the deep breathing of

The Hunt

Maelstrom as he stalked them. They held their breath; fearful they would be just as loud.

Thunder grumbled outside, but the windowless exhibit hall offered no lightning, just deep shadows.

Jake mimed to Lorna to keep moving along the wall. They stealthily passed a display case housing ceramics found in a tomb, and just behind it, a power point. Jake muttered under his breath as he plugged the inconvenient contraption in; hadn't anybody heard of batteries in the eighties?

The screen's old vacuum tube valves warmed up with a faint high-pitched squeal that made Jake cringe. Worse, the phosphorous screen suddenly illuminated like a sickly green torch. Jake just managed to match the blip on the screen to the location in the next room before Maelstrom's grinning face appeared behind the display case, bathed in green light.

'Gotcha!'

Jake didn't hesitate. A plasma sphere jumped from his fingertips—tearing through the display case and exploding in the hero's face. The hero pedalled backwards, clawing at the sparks that burnt his nose. He slammed into a three metre tall statue of Osiris clutching a curved ankh. The relic toppled to the floor. Maelstrom fell amongst the smashed chunks of sandstone, buying Jake and Lorna enough time to cross the hallway.

'Oh no you don't!' roared the hero.

A whirling tornado of air suddenly sprang up next to him, his trademark power. Chunks of stone were sucked up by the powerful twister. Maelstrom pointed at Jake and the whirlwind zigzagged across the hall in pursuit, cannoning through several display cases with no regard for the treasures inside.

Jake had reached the new exhibit hall, displaying stone tablets from the ancient Iraqi empire of Assyria. He had been forced to unplug the scanner again as the power cable was too short, but he was certain what he sought was close by.

The whirlwind screamed through the doorway behind, tearing a chunk of brick from the door jamb. The debris was sucked into the vortex, adding yet more junk to that swirling inside.

'Where now?' shouted Lorna as Jake suddenly stopped in his tracks.

Behind, the whirlwind swayed towards them. She reached out and telekinetically grabbed a two-metre slab depicting King Ashurnasirpal and hurled it at the twister, hoping the weight would extinguish the mini-storm. To her dismay, and with a sense of guilt, the treasured slab was torn asunder by the wind.

Jake got his bearings. 'It's over here—I'm sure of it.'

Beyond an opening in the wall flanked by two huge marble Assyrian *Lammasu*—bulls sporting eagle wings and human heads with depictions of flowing beards—a

The Hunt

smaller Lammasu stood in a tall glass case. This one was much more detailed. The beard of this one didn't share the same ordered symmetry of the others. It was out of place. Jake ran forwards as the mini-tornado sped in pursuit.

Lorna's sneakers suddenly squealed across the stone floor as she found herself no longer able to move forwards—the draught from the tornado was too strong. She angled her body forwards, but still she couldn't break free of the suction.

'Jake!'

Jake hesitated. Lorna was now sliding backwards towards the whirlwind. Huge chunks of stone swirled around inside turning it into a blender that would bludgeon her to death. The whirlwind made a rising-pitch revving sound as it increased speed. Heavy tableaux bolted to the wall suddenly began to swing towards the eye of the storm.

'Fly out!'

'I can't,' screamed Lorna above the powering sound of the wind and the fierce flapping noise of her clothes caught in the gale. 'Help me!'

Jake could feel his clothes and hair being sucked towards the vortex. He took a few firm footsteps towards Lorna, careful not to let the wind sweep him off his feet. Her outstretched hand was centimetres away but he couldn't reach her.

'Closer!'

'I can't,' shouted Jake over the roar. 'It'll pull me right in.'

He suddenly felt the icy claw of the tornado trying to engulf him. His fingers suddenly connected to Lorna's—just as her feet swept out from under her.

Jake braced himself, leaning at a sharp angle away from the tornado. Lorna's feet were sucked into the whirling mass and she howled in pain as the masonry caught within the twister pelted her feet.

'I can't pull you out!'

'Try!'

Jake grunted as he played tug-of-war with Lorna. He made a few centimetres progress . . . then the whirl-wind pounded harder and dragged him backwards.

Lorna kept losing the feeling in her feet until her healing power rebuilt the bones and nerves—only for the detritus trapped in the whirlwind to pound them again. It was a constant cycle of pain.

'Jake . . . please!'

'I won't let go!' He pulled harder—then suddenly felt an arm reach around his neck and yank the Core Power pendant from around his neck. Jake was so surprised, he let go of Lorna—

Lorna was sucked into the cyclone with a scream—that was suddenly silenced as the swaying mass consumed her.

The Hunt

Jake stared at Maelstrom, poised between the two stone bulls guarding the entrance. He was holding the pendant up to the dim emergency lights, a greedy look in his eyes; his broken wings hung from his back, dragging along the ground.

'So it's true . . . ' he whispered in awe. 'They exist.'

'That's not yours! Give it back!' Jake was all too aware of how lame that sounded. It was the kind of remark he was used to at school when he nicked a kid's bag and tossed it between his mates—Big Tony, Scuffer, and Knuckles. Bullies one-and-all.

'Such a treasure doesn't belong in the hands of a child,' scoffed Maelstrom. 'It belongs in the hands of a true hero. One who can see how far astray the Foundation has gone under Kirby's leadership. One who—'

Jake was grateful for the monologue—a sure sign of a true idiot. He summoned the mutated powers in his body to replicate the same telekinetic power Lorna had used—except his manifestation was fuelled by whatever quirk the EMP had done to his body. It made the power much stronger. He motioned to the two marble Lammasu.

Stone cracked as the two bulls tore from their bases, which were bolted into the ground. Each statue weighed several tonnes but moved with fluid grace under Jake's control. Maelstrom just had time to look surprised as the sculptures crashed into him with the solid noise of rock-on-rock.

The whirlwind holding Lorna suddenly vanished and dropped her to the floor in a daze.

Maelstrom's hand, still clutching the pendant, poked out from between the statues. Jake snatched his pendant, placing it back around his neck. With a flick of his wrists he parted the statues, expecting to see a crushed and mangled opponent, but a powerful shield had saved the rogue hero, so his imprint had been left in the statues like a jelly mould. At least he was unconscious.

Lorna climbed onto her knees and reached a wobbling hand for Jake. 'You deliberately let go of me!'

'I had to—'

'You total pig!' screamed Lorna.

Jake didn't know what to say. He turned away and headed for the Lammasu in the other hallway. The display label read that this was a recent gift from Iraq.

'The useless things you learn when you read,' muttered Jake.

Lorna blocked his view, arms akimbo. She wobbled; her head was still spinning from being trapped in the cyclone. 'Don't you ignore me, Jake Hunter.'

'Move.'

'I don't care who you think you are with your creepy pals in the Council of Evil. But you don't treat your

The Hunt

girlfriend like that. Especially if you missed her birth-day!'

Jake opened his mouth to argue, but thought better of it. He gently nudged Lorna aside. By hanging around with him she was putting herself into ever increasing danger. He should leave her for her own good. He felt a guilty twinge for even thinking about that.

He concentrated on the case. His index finger glowed cherry-red and he used it to etch a huge circle in the glass, which melted under the intense heat. He cut an oval large enough to allow him to stand in the case.

'Jake, did you hear what I said?' complained Lorna. She looked pale and was feeling sick.

'Ssshh! This is important,' said Jake, his gaze fixed on the irregular stone bumps that made the statue's beard.

'So am I!'

Jake blotted out Lorna's complaints. He'd had a lot of experience of doing that with his sister, Beth. Jake gently prodded the beard. The stone was all one piece . . . except the irregular bump. With a faint click, a tube ejected out of a small, perfectly carved recess that had been created behind the beard.

With the thrill of discovery, Jake pulled the tube out. It was five centimetres long and made of plastic—clearly a new addition. Lorna poked him in the ribs.

'Are you listening to me?'

Jake wanted to shout at her, but instead tried a conciliatory tone.

'Letting go of you was an accident. And I promise I'll make up for missing your birthday.'

'How?'

Jake had expected to be questioned. He said the first thing that came into his head. 'I'll get you something really rare.'

He turned his attention back to the container, but Lorna was not willing to let the subject drop.

'What's that? What's so important that you let me go when Wind-boy took that necklace of yours?'

Jake prised the plastic container in half. Inside was a rolled up note, hastily written.

'Anyone ever told you that you ask too many questions?'

A chillingly familiar voice answered back: 'And you don't ask enough.'

Jake spun round, shoving Lorna out of the way. Chameleon was standing across the chamber. He was Jake's shape-changing nemesis, currently in his natural form as a pale young man with a dark widow's peak. His face bore the scars of their last few encounters. A long black leather coat hung to his knees, hiding further injuries.

'Didn't you learn to leave me alone, lizard-breath?'

'I'm going to hunt you to extinction.' Chameleon

regarded Lorna with a sneer. 'I see you have a partner in crime these days? Just as I expected.'

'This isn't how it looks,' said Lorna queasily. Then she doubled over and threw up behind the case, her stomach still churning from the intense cyclonic motion.

'Did you think I'd let you, of all people, run wild with a Core Power?'

'So you know?'

'Of course I know,' sneered Chameleon. 'The whole world knows, Hunter. But it won't happen. This time I'm not taking any prisoners.'

'A battle to the death, huh?' Jake tried to sound cocky, but he really didn't want to waste time fighting Chameleon, especially since his powers were acting unpredictably. 'Just how I like it.'

Chameleon's smile was cold and calculating. 'I didn't come alone, Hunter. I brought a mutual friend.'

There was movement in the darkness and another figure appeared. Jake's heart missed a beat. It was a foe who wanted him dead. A foe who had no memory of him.

She was known as the Reaper.

She was Jake's sister . . . and the expression on her face was baying for blood.

'You tried to kill my parents, Hunter. Bad idea.'

Compounded Complications

Jake edged round the display case. It was a flimsy shield between his sister and Chameleon, but he didn't want to start a fight. He talked fast. The edge of nervousness in his voice was something he wasn't used to.

'Beth . . . I'm your brother! They were our parents! I saved them because these guys—him—the Foundation, did something bad to them. They stole their memories, like they did to you!'

'I've heard all this nonsense before and it didn't work then!'

Chameleon smiled smugly. Beth raised her arms in a superpowered Kung-fu stance. Jake couldn't help but notice that a hand was missing, a hand that he had severed.

Jake held up his hands in a desperate plea for calm. 'No, no, no . . . think about it. Why don't your parents want to see you any more?'

Beth hesitated. There was a flicker of uncertainty in

her eyes. She recited the excuse Chameleon had given her. 'Because it's too dangerous for me to be around them. I'm protecting them.'

'No. They think you've gone off the rails. They think you have turned into what I used to be.' *Still am*, he added mentally. 'They think you're a bully, into gangs or something. They're upset because of it. I see them regularly, Beth. When was the last time you did?'

Beth lowered her hands. Chameleon snarled, and stood in front of her, breaking her eye contact with Jake.

'Enough of this trash!'

WHAM! A fireball jumped from his hands—obliterating the display case between them. The stone Lammasu statue deflected the blast from Jake.

Furious, Jake returned the volley. A jet of napalm-like fire shot from his hands—but it was nothing more than a trickle, like the last dregs in a water pistol. It splashed down short of his mark. Jake hid back round the statue and gawped at his hands; now was not the time for his powers to act up.

'Hit me, and you'll destroy the pendant!' shouted Jake.

'I don't think so, Hunter. They're practically indestructible! I can take it from whatever pieces of your body remain.'

Jake's heart sank; accidental damage to the pendant

Compounded Complications

was his only trump card. Chameleon fired again. This time the Lammasu splintered apart in a shower of rubble.

'I think that was priceless!' shouted Lorna.

'Shut up, traitor!' bellowed Chameleon as he hurled a fireball at her feet. The ground shattered, throwing Lorna into a wall.

Jake sprinted across the hall as he tried to put as much distance as he could between him and the heroes. He hid behind a large stone fresco depicting an ancient battle. He searched around for an escape route, but the windowless room felt more like a tomb.

He noticed Lorna was groaning, but otherwise unhurt. She was extra baggage he didn't want to deal with now. However, it was apparent that Chameleon thought she had swapped sides and even Jake was unsure where her allegiances lay. In fact, Chameleon was acting oddly: he would normally be worried about preserving the artefacts in the room, but he was destroying them with careless abandonment.

Beth suddenly somersaulted over the fresco and landed in front of Jake. He opened his mouth to speak—but she booted him hard in the chest.

The super-strength kick forced Jake backwards through the fresco. He felt like a football as his trajectory lifted him diagonally up across the hall and into the ceiling, which he dented with a shower of plaster

dust before plummeting back to earth. A plate glass display case and priceless pots broke his fall.

Beth charged across the hallway, her boots clacking on the stone floor. Jake shook his groggy head to try and focus his mind. He noticed he was now opposite an archway that led deeper into the museum.

Lorna appeared in the corner of his vision and shot a stream of ice across Beth's path. The Reaper slipped; her momentum carried her into the base of a statue.

Jake used the distraction and ran for the archway. Lorna had saved him again—but in doing so had put her own life on the line. He felt another pang of conscience for dragging her into such danger. He knew it had to stop.

Chameleon hurled more fireballs that ignited the wall as Jake ran towards the exit. The arch looked like a hoop of fire by the time Jake charged through.

The flames triggered the smoke alarm. Jake had assumed Maelstrom had disconnected the phone lines and alarm circuits, but the smoke detectors must have been on a separate loop.

The siren whooped around the hall and a stream of carbon dioxide plumed from the sprinklers. Water would damage the exhibits.

Jake ran through the new hall, ignoring the exhibits, and reached yet another, deeper into the bowels of the building. He was completely lost. Terrifying childhood memories started coming back. Unseen terrors lurking in the pitch black.

He struggled to put them out of his mind and repeated to himself: *I'm the most terrifying thing in the museum.*

He paid attention to his surroundings. That was the only way he would escape. The flames from the archway illuminated a large model next to him. It was a Greek temple with detailed mural below—the *Neried Monument*.

Jake didn't have time to admire the craftsmanship as, throughout the museum, solid fire doors started to descend from the roof. They were designed to make each section of the building fireproof, preventing damage from spreading amongst the priceless exhibits. He ran ahead—but something forcefully collided into his back, making him drop the plastic case. It skittered into the hallway beyond.

'Struggling will just make me angrier!' snarled Chameleon as he sat on Jake's back, pinning him down.

'So you got me. You going to try and arrest me again? Maybe I can add a few extra scars to your face if you do.' Jake was referring to the last time Chameleon had him prisoner in the Foundation's maximum-security prison block, carved from an iceberg. Jake had easily escaped from that, just as he had escaped from Diablo Island.

Chameleon tore the pendant from around Jake's neck.

'Not this time. I'm not taking the risk. There's no way you can be allowed to retrieve the Core Power. I've authorized the use of extreme-force on this one, Hunter. Do you know what that means?'

The fire doors sealed the exits and the carbon dioxide gas rapidly filled the room. In a minute they would both choke to death.

'Killing me will make you just as much a villain as anyone at the Council. Kirby wouldn't let that happen and that's not your style.'

'My style has changed. And Kirby? Ha!' Chameleon spat. 'He has displayed a shocking lack of leadership at the Foundation while you have got under my skin and compounded the problems we have been having. Eliminating you is the only option left . . . and I'm going to take great delight in doing it.'

Chameleon's hands squeezed around his throat. Jake choked. He had to concentrate to invoke what powers were still working.

He apported—appearing behind Chameleon, as the hero collapsed on the floor. Jake pinned Chameleon down, reversing the position they had both been in seconds ago. He pushed the hero's face against the floor and snatched the pendant back.

Chameleon thrashed around, transforming into his

Compounded Complications

bipedal lizard form. Jake held on, using his knees to pin Chameleon's arms. The shapeshifter's thrashing tail coiled around Jake's neck.

Jake's fingers glowed with the same heat he had used to melt the glass. He gripped Chameleon's tail and yanked it free. The hero howled in pain as his skin burned.

'I could kill you right now,' hissed Jake. 'But unlike you, I have style.'

Without another word, he apported into the room beyond, leaving Chameleon in the enclosed space that was quickly filling up with a deadly gas.

Jake appeared in a new hall, just beyond the fire door. It was another long hall, filled with Greek sculptures. This room was filling with CO_2 gas as well. Jake blindly searched for the plastic tube through the heavy gas undulating on the floor. His fingers fell upon the tube as the door behind him exploded open, Beth poised in the doorframe.

'There's a reason I'm not fighting you, Beth. Don't you think that's odd?'

He saw his sister hesitate and hoped he was getting through to her . . . but then her lip curled into a snarl. Jake didn't want to wait around any longer. He apported from the room—

Appearing in the rainy street outside. Jake suddenly realized that he had left Lorna alone inside, with the two rampaging heroes. He felt guilty, and knew he couldn't smooth-talk his way out of this one, but there was no way he was going back to rescue her.

He had to leave her. As much as it hurt them both, he was doing it for her own good.

Approaching fire engine sirens howled across the city. Jake tried to open a quantum tunnel, but his power spluttered, opening up a small circle in the air through which he could see his warm dry Council chamber beyond, before the hole quickly sealed itself.

Jake ran down the street, pulling his phone from his pocket. He dropped Leech's chunky scanner in a rubbish bin, then chose the teleport power to download from Villain.net.

Jake turned into an alleyway. To the few passers-by, the thunderclap from his teleportation sounded like part of the storm.

The sound of air-conditioning units was overwhelming in the room, forcing any conversation to be carried out by shouting. An engineer, dressed in casual jeans and a T-shirt, carefully laid the optical processor in the specially designed zero-insertion-force, or ZIF, tray, and gently locked it in place. His fingers trembled as he had never before held such a leap in technology. He looked at Pete standing across the room and waited for him to nod,

Compounded Complications

before he slid the tray into the belly of the computer system that Forge had spent stolen millions building.

Pete watched as the huge computer powered up, loading a bespoke operating system that worked with the new processor. Finally, after painful minutes of waiting, a screen flicked to life with the basic OS interface. Pete smiled, but his cracked cheeks stung from the movement.

'It works!' exclaimed the scientist.

'Good,' shouted Pete over the noisy fans needed to cool the computer. He examined a photocopied sheet his army of researchers had uncovered. They had spent weeks trying to discover everything they could about the Core Power and, although they still did not know its nature, they had found references to it, hidden in a volume in the Library of Congress in Washington DC. It was a series of symbols, the same symbols carved on the tips of the pendants. The researchers learned that they were part of a complex mathematical code that dictated how the pendant should be assembled.

All he had to do was use the computer's impressive capabilities to hack into the Foundation's encrypted servers to steal the solution to how the pendant fitted together. He knew they had it, they were the ones who had created the pendants in the first place.

All he then had to do was get the pendants.

'Start the hack,' he ordered.

The scientist activated the program and sat back as numbers crunched across the screen. Pete didn't hear the door open behind him and nervously jumped when Orsina appeared next to him.

'We have a message through,' she shouted.

Pete held up his hand as text started appearing on the screen.

Orsina nudged him again. 'Pete, you should really listen to this.'

'It's working,' exclaimed Pete. 'The processor has given us enough power to breach the Foundation's firewall! This is all the information they have on the Core Power Hunter is looking for.'

Pete coughed as he read the data, ignoring the trickle of blood on his lips. After he had fallen ill, a medical scan revealed it was because of an artificial virus Jake had placed inside him. Pete recognized it instantly, it was similar to the one Momentum had asked him to create to infect Jake's parents. Jake had used his own powers to adapt it and had planted it back into Pete . . . and it was slowly killing him.

The hope that the Core Power could help cure him, or that he could at least use it as a bargaining chip to persuade Jake to cure him, was now Pete's primary goal.

Having to face the possibility of his own death was a sobering thought, and it made all other concerns with

Compounded Complications

Forge seem irrelevant. The bitterness he had felt against his parents vanished in an instant, replaced with longings to see them again, and the resentful chips he had been carrying against his old friends, such as Toby, melted away.

He now saw that life was just too precious to waste on spite.

'Wow . . . ' cried Pete as he read the secret report on the screen outlining the history of the Core Power: how it had been taken from a villain by a hero called Leech. Leech had been in no hurry to relinquish such power and had gone on a rampage that had nearly brought about the end of the world. The Foundation and Council had united to rip the power from Leech and cast him into exile.

'Do you know what the power is?' he yelled to Orsina. He tapped the screen. Orsina stared at the answer on the screen and shrugged. Pete huffed in annoyance. 'That . . . is one of the most powerful powers . . . in the universe. What do you think will happen if Hunter has that?'

Pete swayed—half from a weakness that swept over his body, half from the sudden realization of what horror lay ahead.

Orsina tugged his sleeve, pulling him from his daze.

'Pete—I get it, I really do. But something has turned up that needs your immediate attention.'

Pete dragged his gaze away from the screen.

'OK, that's enough,' he ordered the engineer. 'Shut it down before they trace us. Start the calculations on the symbols. I want to know how to use this power once we get it.'

'Pete,' Orsina prompted impatiently.

Pete nodded and followed her out of the room. He was feeling much older, decades older, than he should. Whether that was an effect of the virus inside him, or from what he had just read, he didn't know.

Not only did he have to face the prospect of dying; he now had the possibility that Jake could bring about the end of the world.

Jake Hunter had to be stopped at all costs. He would have to devote every resource Forge had to stop him.

Jake teleported into his chamber at the Council of Evil. For some reason, his calculations were off as he appeared near the ceiling and crashed down on top of his desk. Jake groaned from the pain that shot through his leg—his healing power had mysteriously vanished during the teleportation. That wasn't right. He needed to get himself examined. But first, he had something more pressing to attend to.

He rubbed his shin as he dropped into his seat and emptied his pockets, producing the pendant with the now broken cord, his mobile phone, and the plastic container he had retrieved from the museum.

Licking his fingers, Jake clicked open the two halves of the cylinder and unrolled the paper inside. Leech had assured him that it would reveal the location of the Core Power's next section.

It was a handwritten diary fragment, although nothing made sense as Jake couldn't work out the context of the message. He couldn't see the vaguest hint of a location. Doodles and numbers covered the margins. Jake read quickly through, but there was nothing obvious. Irritated, he read more slowly. It had been written by a hero called Avenger. He had found himself hunted by a supervillain, led by Fallout—one of the surviving Council members. Fallout had used dozens of villains to lure out and attack Avenger. Jake sympathized with that.

The hero had been injured, but still managed to slip through Fallout's clutches. However, the wound he had sustained was not healing and he knew he didn't have much time left. He vowed he'd sacrifice himself if it meant keeping the pendant hidden from the Council. He planned to hide the pendant and leave the marker capsule so others from the Foundation could find it.

Jake flipped the paper over. There was nothing on the back. No mention of where Avenger had hidden it.

The white space on the paper had been filled with numbers, scrubbed out words and doodles.

'Useless,' muttered Jake.

He reclined in his chair and thought hard. Perhaps where Avenger had hidden the message was a clue? He'd hidden it in a statue in the British Museum . . .

No . . . he'd hidden it in the statue which, according to the display label Jake had glanced at, was recently discovered in an archaeological dig in Iraq. The Middle East. That was a start.

Jake's phone rang. He glanced at the cracked screen—it was an unknown number, probably his mum. He cradled the phone against his ear with his shoulder as he re-read the message.

'Hello?'

WHAM! Lorna materialized through the phone—sending him sprawling against the desk and forcing him to drop his phone again. The already cracked screen shattered on impact.

Jake stared at Lorna with fury . . . but the angry look on her face cautioned him against saying anything.

'You coward!' she yelled, poking him in the chest with her finger. 'You left me back there with those two maniacs!'

'I . . . you . . . they're on your side. I thought you'd be safe with them.'

'Liar!'

Compounded Complications

'Seriously! You're all heroes together, right?'

'Chameleon has flipped. You saw him. He's not looking for that pendant of yours for the Foundation. He wants it for himself.'

Jake was sceptical. 'I hate the guy, but I don't think he would do that. He's not the type to flip. And he called you a traitor.'

Lorna jabbed him in the ribs again. 'Exactly! He thinks I'm on your side now! And he is most definitely on his *own* side. He thinks Kirby has lost it at the Foundation and wants to declare all-out war against the Council!'

Jake was about to respond—but suddenly stopped. 'The Council!' he exclaimed.

'What about it?'

A chill ran down Jake's spine. Lorna had just appeared inside the Council of Evil's top-secret headquarters. She was still classed as a hero. If she was found she would be killed, and Jake would be held accountable for bringing her here. His voice dropped to a whisper.

'This is the Council! You're not supposed to be here. The coordinates of this place are secret and . . . ' he trailed off as something else occurred to him.

Fear spread across Lorna's face as she realized where she was. The internal messenger on Jake's computer suddenly bonged for attention.

'Don't say a word,' he hissed. He answered the impatiently bouncing messenger icon on his screen. He cleared his throat and kept his voice level. 'What is it?'

'Necros wants to see you, Hunter. Now, in his chamber.'

The line went dead. Jake's mouth felt parched. He had never been summoned to Necros's chamber before. It wasn't a good sign.

'Does he know I'm here?' asked Lorna nervously.

Jake shook his head. 'I don't think so . . . '

He had brought Pete back to the COE once, and nobody had known until he presented him to Necros. Momentum had successfully kidnapped Lorna's brother, Toby, and brought him here without anybody knowing.

'What do we do?'

Jake ignored her and called up an online world map. When he had mentioned coordinates to Lorna, he had had a sudden flash of inspiration. He entered the string of numbers on Avenger's note.

On-screen, the globe spun round and a location was highlighted.

'They are coordinates . . . latitude and longitude,' he said to himself. 'Avenger left a GPS trail.'

'What are you talking about? Jake? Look, you better start telling me what's going on.'

Compounded Complications

Jake looked at her. If Necros had heard the rumours that were circulating about Jake hunting for the Core Power, then he would try and stop him. If Jake fled now, it was a clear sign of guilt. But surely Necros would be banging down Jake's door if he suspected him?

'Security . . . ' he mumbled.

'Jake, you're not making sense.'

Jake's heart sank. Necros knew Lorna was here. He must do. Hiding her would be the worst thing he could do.

'Since a Council member was assassinated on the island, Necros increased security and deployed the Duradan . . . '

'Dura-what?'

'The Duradan. They're, like, royal guards. They're highly trained soldiers whose job is to protect the Council members. They locked down every entrance to the island; the docks, the airstrip, everything. That included teleporting, quantum tunnelling . . . just about every form of travel possible. High-ranking officials, like me, are allowed to come and go as we want—but the Duradan would have detected you entering the island. They know you're here!'

Lorna blanched. She had just walked into the lion's den.

Jake thought back to a piece of advice he had been

given about chess. Always think several moves ahead of your opponent. It had worked for him before.

He smiled at Lorna. 'Lorn . . . I have an idea. But I don't think you're going to like it.'

'Like what? I don't like the expression on your face for a start.'

'You're going to meet Necros. And you're going to be my prisoner.'

Pete stared at the visitor in surprise. It was the last person he had expected to see . . . well, maybe not the last, but . . .

'Hi, Pete. You've changed somewhat since we last met.'

'And you look . . . more beaten up,' said Pete cautiously.

Chameleon smiled. He remained seated across the table, drinking from a bottle of water Orsina had given him.

'Er . . . you do realize where you are, right?' said Pete.

'Sure. Forge, right? Nice place you've set up. I like the Rocky Mountains. Very relaxing. Some good fishing around here.'

Pete didn't feel like a casual chat, not after what he had just discovered. 'What are you doing here?'

'That was blunt.'

Compounded Complications

'That was to the point. I take it you think you're going to stop Forge?'

Chameleon burst out laughing. 'Stop Forge? Why would I possibly want to do that?'

Pete was surprised. 'Because it's the usual poncy do-gooder thing you like to do, and because the Hero Foundation sees us as a threat.'

The smile left Chameleon's face instantly. 'The Foundation? Pete, as we speak, the world is falling apart. Across America and a lot of Europe there are massive power outages because of something Eric Kirby let happen. Kirby has run the Foundation into the ground. He has destroyed its potential. He sees everybody as a threat.'

'But we are,' said Pete, more for his own pride than trying to prove a point.

'Of course you are. Because you have made Forge the only logical choice between the Foundation and the Council.'

Chameleon stood up and began pacing. Orsina reacted nervously, acidic drops dripping from her fingers in anticipation of a fight. Chameleon ignored her. His brow was creased as he spoke.

'Why do you think Primes and Downloaders have been coming to you? OK, at first you were nothing but a bunch of trouble causers nobody took seriously . . . but now, now you have a force at your fingertips that could really change the world . . . and save it while Kirby leads the Foundation into crisis. Are you aware of what the Council are doing? Specifically your old foe, Jake Hunter?'

'He's collecting parts of a Core Power.'

Chameleon hesitated, surprised by Pete's answer. He pulled himself together.

'That's right. And you know what it does?' Pete nodded. 'Then you know why that can't happen? Why it should be in safer hands?'

'Yours?'

'*Ours*. The Foundation is mixed up in other chaotic business of its own creation. They are dying under Kirby's leadership. With Forge we can stop Hunter. If we work together.'

Pete felt a wave of nausea twist his stomach, not from Chameleon's suggestion, but from his growing illness. Pete wasn't interested in the Core Power, just Jake. And if he could use Chameleon to help him achieve that . . .

Pete held out his hand. Chameleon looked at the flaking bluish skin and thought twice about shaking it.

'If you want Forge's help, then we have a deal. A truce.'

Chameleon smiled, which faltered slightly as he took Pete's disgusting hand and shook it.

Compounded Complications

* * *

Necros stared at Lorna cowering on the floor.

'A spy you say?' he said in his sonorous voice.

The echo was dampened by the darkness surrounding them. Since Jake had entered the fiend's personal chamber he had been unable to see anything. Necros sat on an obsidian throne, lit by a light source Jake couldn't pinpoint. It was as if the room absorbed all the light, only illuminating what Necros wanted it to. There was a powerful odour of decay.

'She was one of Kirby's top Downloaders,' said Jake. He didn't want to look at Lorna. The stricken fear on her face might trigger his own. His legs were trembling under Necros's gaze. He still didn't know why he had been summoned. Perhaps the Council leader had discovered who was behind the spate of recent Council member assassinations?

Jake cast those troubling thoughts aside. He didn't want to give Necros any hints to his own guilt. He hoped his scam with Lorna would deflect attention from him.

'Did she not help you escape from the Foundation's hospital?' asked Necros.

That meant Necros was aware what the Foundation were accusing her of. Jake thought it best not to lie; or at least not to twist the story too far from the facts.

'She was of help, but she didn't do it willingly. I leeched the powers from her to escape. She didn't know what hit her.' Jake tried to sound smug.

Necros remained silent. He wore a deep hood that hid his face. Jake had never seen it, and couldn't tell if the villain was looking at him or Lorna.

'You leeched them,' repeated Necros.

Lorna struggled against the plastic ties that bound her wrists. She screamed, but the tape that gagged her muffled the noise. She hadn't been at all happy when Jake had done that.

'And you say she was following you?'

'Yes. Spying on me for the Foundation.'

Necros made a rumbling noise in the back of his throat. 'And *what* exactly were you doing?'

Jake hesitated; regretting that he'd just re-focused the conversation on himself. 'I was trying to find Forge.' It was as good an excuse as any. Before Jake had started his campaign against the Council leaders, they had tasked Jake to find and destroy Forge. 'And I think she can help. After all, she used to be good friends with Pete Kendall.'

Silence poured from Necros's throne.

Jake fidgeted. Did Necros know what he was really doing? His eyes suddenly fell on the pendant hanging around the villain's neck. Leech had warned him that getting that piece would be more difficult than

Compounded Complications

obtaining the one around Eric Kirby's neck—and that would be no walk in the park. Jake had decided to chase the two most difficult parts last of all; at least he knew where they were.

Finally, Necros spoke up. 'These are dangerous times for us, Hunter. We have had recruits leaving us to join Forge. With the Council leaders mercilessly struck down, we have weakened as an organization. It is difficult to know who to trust. To know who plots against the Council. Especially those schemers on our side.'

Silence again.

Every nerve in Jake was screaming that Necros knew about his betrayals. Jake felt the villain was like a cat playing with a mouse before killing it. Jake found his voice.

'I agree. That's why I want to use Lorna to strike back at Forge. Kill the competition.' The pursuing silence unnerved Jake even more. 'Um . . . why did you want to see me?'

'I'm seeing all the remaining Council leaders. I have to know who I can trust.' He pointed a finger, covered by a black metal glove, at Lorna. 'I see from this that you are active in your pursuits. I want you to continue, Hunter. You have everything at the Council at your disposal. Complete your mission!'

Jake released a pent-up laugh. Necros had just, unknowingly, given him the run of the Council's facilities to find the Core Powers—all under the pretence of destroying Forge.

It was a stroke of luck.

He yanked Lorna to her feet and she viciously kicked him. He knew the moment the gag was released, he would be in trouble—but it had been worth it. Lorna's presence had just won him the support of the most feared villain in the world.

'Where does your task take you next?' enquired Necros.

Jake didn't see the need to lie. He had unscrambled the coordinates on Avenger's marker. He knew where he must go. Avenger had hidden the pendant, then lured the pursuing villains around the globe before he had the opportunity to deposit his clue inside the statue while in Iraq. With the coordinates, Avenger's route around the world had been made clear.

'I have a lead in China.'

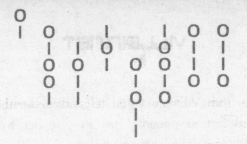

China

Soft fog draped across the forest flanking either side of the large stone wall Jake appeared on. It took him a moment to adjust to the spectacle of the wall zigzagging across the forest-carpeted hills; rising and falling like a rollercoaster track, punctuated by watchtowers on the highest peaks that were now silhouettes in the morning fog. The section of wall he stood on climbed steeply in a series of worn steps to the nearest watchtower.

The scale of the Great Wall of China impressed even Jake, and he was seldom moved by anything. It was a colossal engineering feat. His eye started to water, not from any emotional reaction, but because Lorna had punched him, giving him a black eye that no amount of his healing power would shift. Another sign his powers were behaving oddly.

Lorna refused to look at him, instead she looked out from the battlements. The moment he had returned to his Council chamber she had struck him, launching into a screaming fit of obscenities. Jake had downloaded powers from Villain.net and teleported them out of there as fast as possible, just in case her hysterics brought some unwelcome attention.

Jake felt a little guilty, but the benefits of bluffing Necros outweighed the tantrum. 'You can go home if you like.' He saw Lorna's shoulders bunch with tension. 'I'll call you when I get back,' he added lamely.

His words were dampened by the fog, which made Lorna's silence all the more damning.

'I don't want you here.' The moment he said it, he regretted the clumsy words. He had meant it to sound friendlier.

Lorna spun round, furious. 'You don't want me here? You ungrateful little . . .' words failed her. 'You wouldn't be here if it wasn't for me! And what thanks do I get? You haul me in front of that super-creep as your prisoner?'

'I—'

'You miss my birthday; you drop me in the middle of a twister and leave me at the mercy of two crazy idiots. And just when I think you can't get any lower, Jake, you surpass expectations! What's wrong with you?'

'This is—'

'You know, I may have been out of the loop at the Foundation, but I've heard all the rumours about you. You're after some kind of ultimate weapon. Is that true? Do you really think you're mature enough to handle that?'

Jake found himself up against the battlement; he hadn't been aware Lorna was forcing him backwards.

'Well?' she asked impatiently.

'It's something called a Core Power . . .'

'I know, I got Emily to look it up for me on the Foundation's wiki. It's a legend. It doesn't exist.'

Jake pulled out the pendant from his pocket. He had secured the broken cord to his jean's belt loop so it couldn't fall out. He had no idea why he trusted Lorna so much, maybe because she had just given him a black eye.

'That's what they want you to think. This is it. Or at least . . . part of it. One of six.'

The sight of it stopped Lorna's tirade. 'The others?'

'I have . . . more of them. The piece I'm looking for is around here somewhere. Hidden by a Prime who was guarding it. If I get that, I can lock what I have together and start using the power. I need all six to get full control.'

Lorna's eyes hadn't left the pendant. 'You're dealing with forces way beyond anything we download.' Jake slid the pendant back into his pocket. 'Do you even know what it does?'

'No. But whatever it is, this is my last fight. Both the Foundation and the Council are going down. They've both used me enough and ruined my life. They're not going to do it after today.'

'Destroying the Council, I understand . . . kind of. I mean, technically, you're one of them. But destroying the Foundation? That doesn't make sense. They're . . . we're the good guys.'

'You saw what they did to my family; to my sister. And then they go and block you from using Hero.com. I used to think there was a line between good and bad, but now I know there's not. The only difference is the name; the attitudes are the same and the winners call themselves the heroes. Everybody's after this Core Power now. Everybody, the good, the bad, and the ugly.'

Lorna laughed. 'I must have hit you very hard, huh? What you're saying is nonsense.'

Her flippant comment irked Jake. He wasn't prepared to argue the virtues of heroes over villains.

'Forget it. You don't understand.'

Lorna's expression darkened. 'You're pathetic, Jake. I've stood by you ever since I knew what you were. "Dark Hunter"? Did you ever think that was a hero's name?'

'I didn't choose it. The Foundation did, Eric Kirby, to be exact. I told you, the only difference in side, is the name.'

Lorna shook her head, searching for the words. 'You

China

know . . . I . . . I used to like you. I used to think you were not the moron you pretended to be. I should have listened to Em and Pete . . . they were right about you.' She looked at him levelly in the eye. 'I helped you when you needed it. And when I needed help, somebody to talk to . . . you made me your prisoner.'

'I did that to save your life! You would have been killed if anybody found you! That was quick thinking on my part.'

'And my birthday?'

'That again? You said you were OK about that! You understood that I was too busy . . . '

Lorna's voice dropped to a whisper. 'We're over, Jake. I don't want to be your girlfriend. I don't want to see you again.'

Jake waited for the tears . . . but they didn't emerge. Lorna just looked sad.

'Then go,' he said quietly. He didn't want her to go, but at least she would be safer away from him.

'I can't. My powers expired back in your "office".' She held up her mobile phone—a message on the screen read: 'USER BLOCKED'. 'I guess Toby realized his phone was missing so I can't even log-on to Hero.com. You're going to have to drop me back home.'

Jake opened his mouth to make an angry comment— but stopped himself. He couldn't let this new development stop his quest. He was surprised to discover how upset he felt about being dumped. He drew a long breath and pulled a GPS from his pocket. He studied the screen, refusing to meet Lorna's gaze.

'I'll do it when I've finished here.'

The GPS screen wasn't like the usual ones found in cars, displaying street names and local features. It was an arrow and a string of longitude and latitude coordinates. Jake slowly turned round until the arrow was pointing straight at the watchtower closest to them.

Lorna followed Jake up the crumbling steps. The incline was so steep that they were forced to use their hands to climb up. Brickwork crumbled under their weight, and the proliferation of moss and weeds between the cracks indicated that tourists did not visit this section of the wall.

Jake and Lorna reached the watchtower's entrance. Inside was a hall and another archway that led to the continuing wall. The location on the GPS was inside the building.

'This is it?' asked Lorna.

'This is where Avenger hid it.'

'Why did he hide it?'

'A lot of people were chasing him for it. He had nowhere to turn.'

'Did they get him?'

'Eventually.'

China

'And you don't think that tale is similar to your own? Get the pendant, then a bunch of crazies come hunting you down.'

'The difference is, I'm much smarter than he was.'

Jake stepped into the tower. Lorna sniggered. The way she was feeling right now, she couldn't think of anyone dumber.

She followed him inside, suddenly wondering what kind of person follows an idiot . . .

Their eyes quickly adjusted to the dim light. It was quite a spacious hall, which would have once housed dozens of men. The remains of a wooden ladder led up to a higher level that was partitioned by rotting floor-boards.

Jake carefully examined the stone flags on the floor. The cracks were filled with old dirt; none of them looked as if they'd been moved in centuries.

'It could be anywhere,' huffed Lorna.

'He was in a hurry . . . so it can't be that well hidden.'

'Maybe somebody else found it?'

'We would have heard about it. Wait here.'

Jake gently levitated up through the opening in the ceiling; he had downloaded flying, but for some reason, the power wouldn't stick.

The top floor of the tower was in dire need of restoration. The floorboards groaned under his weight as he gently alighted. A ragged hole in the wall offered a view across the foggy forest. There was nothing here of immediate interest to Jake.

Below, Lorna tried her weight on the remains of the rotting ladder. It collapsed under her weight, pitching her to the floor.

'Jake!'

'Will you shut up for a minute?' he muttered low enough for her not to hear.

Jake stepped towards the hole in the wall. The edges of the bricks were charred. He traced long black scorch marks on the sidewall, all evidence of a super-powered fight.

'Jake!' came Lorna's voice from below. He ignored her. There was another trapdoor leading to the roof.

Jake levitated under it and gently pressed against the damp wooden door. It wouldn't budge, it was blocked from above. He tried harder—then he shouldered the wood with his improved strength. The timbers splintered away and he drifted out onto the roof.

He touched down on firm stone flags. A battlement ran around the rooftop, offering views in every direction, although he could see little through the thickening fog. He glanced over the edge, noticing the watchtower was built on the peak of a rocky pinnacle.

Where could the pendant be hidden? Somewhere a casual passerby wouldn't discover it . . .

China

He concentrated on summoning his internal super-powers; the ones that had made him the secret weapon everybody wanted; the ones that could create any superpower just by thinking about it . . .

Nothing happened.

He tried again, a sense of panic growing in the pit of his stomach. His powers had been acting peculiarly ever since the EMP had scrambled them. But now it looked as though his worst fears had come to fruition— he had lost his special abilities!

There was a part of him that knew this; but the rest of him struggled to accept it. Without his powers, he felt as if he was an ordinary boy again . . . not even an average villain, but just a kid who no longer had part of him entangled with Villain.net.

He was no longer special.

His stomach churned. If he had to rely on Villain.net then that left him as weak as Lorna—the downloaded powers could disappear at any time.

He pulled out his mobile phone, and selected the power he needed without a second thought. The brick battlements around him suddenly became grey and opaque as he peered through them with his X-ray vision. He glanced at his own pocket. He could see through the denim, his skin and muscles, right through to the bone beneath. If the metal pendant was around, it would be clearly visible as a dark shape the X-rays

couldn't penetrate. Now he knew exactly what he was looking for.

He glanced around the roof. Nothing appeared to be concealed in the walls. He extended his gaze down to the level below, the level beneath his feet vanishing as his gaze bore deeper. There was nothing there either. He was beginning to feel frustrated. Had he got the message wrong? Where the numbers not coordinates after all?

He could see Lorna through the transparent floor. She was acting oddly—backing away from something . . .

He adjusted the strength of his X-ray vision and saw a pair of figures enter the watchtower. They moved threateningly towards Lorna. Jake now realized that Lorna had been trying to get his attention to warn him. There was no mistaking who they were—Chameleon and his sister.

How had they found him?

He saw Beth roughly grab Lorna. Lorna shouted again. This time there was no mistaking the anguish in her voice.

'Jake!'

He had to think fast. There was no use pretending he wasn't here. 'Hold on a minute. I think I've found it.' That lie might buy him an extra minute. 'I'll be right down.'

China

He was stuck. Chameleon had somehow followed him here, and now had Lorna as a prisoner. The hero was clearly not averse to using her as a bargaining chip.

Jake thought through his options. He could leave Lorna to fend for herself again, but that would ruin any chance he had of patching things up with her. The perilous situation made him realize just how selfish his actions towards her had been—even if he had intended to do the right thing. Lorna could have left him to fend for himself numerous times before, but she'd always stood by his side. He should do the same.

She was right about Chameleon's unusual behaviour. The shapeshifter was a Prime, born with his powers. Jake had heard warnings about Primes who had mixed their own powers with those downloaded from Villain.net. Some had turned crazy, others had died. He suspected Chameleon had been downloading powers from Hero.com to help him on his quest.

'Almost got it . . . ' he absently shouted down as he turned off his X-ray vision and scrolled through Villain.net. He quickly found some familiar icons. In times of crisis, he wanted to put his trust in his old favourite powers. He downloaded them.

'OK. I'm coming down!'

* * *

Lorna felt Beth's grip tighten around her wrists. The message was clear: don't raise the alarm.

'How can you do this to your own brother?' hissed Lorna.

Beth frowned. 'What?'

'Jake's your brother. You must remember?'

Lorna was satisfied with the puzzled look that crossed Beth's face. There was a thump from overhead, and footsteps walking across the creaking floorboards.

Jake shouted down, 'Lorn, I got the pendant!' The unusually cheerful tone in his voice alerted Lorna that he was trying to dupe their unwelcome guests.

Beth tightened her grip on Lorna and edged towards the corner so she wouldn't be immediately visible when Jake dropped into the room. Chameleon hung back in another corner, coiled ready to strike.

'I'm coming down!'

Chameleon was so tense he was ready to break. The anticipation caused the veins in his neck to twitch.

Only Lorna noticed Jake silently levitate down outside the archway they had entered through. He must have dropped outside from the level above. His hands were glowing a brilliant green. He opened fire before his feet touched the wall.

Radioactive green streamers lashed from his fingers and struck Chameleon in the back.

Lorna used the distraction to elbow Beth in the solar

plexus. She grunted, releasing Lorna. Lorna sprinted towards Jake for protection, ducking as he hurled another volley of neon green that forced Beth through the opposite archway and down the steps beyond.

Beth rolled end-over-end, the wind knocked from her as she rapidly slid down the crumbling stairway. She was unconscious when she hit the bottom.

Jake's eyes became mirrored as he activated his X-ray vision and swept the room. The pendant wasn't hidden in the walls or floor . . . he glanced up and saw it hidden in a hastily carved recess in the ceiling joist above. He reached up for it—

'Watch out!'

Lorna flung herself at Jake, grabbing him around the waist and into a corner as Chameleon blasted a fireball from his prone position on the floor. It exploded against the wall, giving the shapeshifter enough time to acrobatically flip to his feet—transforming into his lizard form as he did so. His tail had regenerated, in part because of his healing power, and partly because of his inherited lizard traits.

Chameleon scampered under the beam Jake had been reaching for and looked inquisitively at it. He spotted the fake panel.

Jake pushed Lorna aside and bellowed with rage. Another radioactive strand shot from his hand. The energy whip coiled around Chameleon's waist just as he removed the panel—revealing a small cloth-bound object.

Jake had no choice but to pull Chameleon towards him to stop him from snatching the bundle. Jake swung a punch—but the hero was expecting it and effortlessly caught Jake's fist.

Both warriors' arms trembled as their super-strength vied for supremacy.

Lorna watched the stalemate. Her hand suddenly fell onto Jake's mobile phone. It must have dropped from his pocket when she pulled him aside. The screen was illuminated, displaying Villain.net.

She stared at it . . .

Chameleon's tail swung out, sweeping Jake off his feet. The energy whip coiled off the hero. For a couple of seconds, he didn't know what to do—then he came to his senses and snagged the cloth bundle from the recess.

'Mine!' Chameleon hesitated, wondering if he should finish Jake off or escape with his prize. 'You lose, Hunter.'

It was just the pause in action Lorna was waiting for.

Chameleon never saw the water jet spray from her palms. Two fine jets sprayed with the force of a police cannon. Chameleon was slammed against the masonry, dislodging the ancient bricks.

The cloth bundle fell. Pools of water sloshed across

the floor and carried it towards the archway on its own miniature whitewater ride.

Jake scrambled after it—but the torrent of water flowed down the steep steps like a rapid and the cloth swept down with it . . . towards where Beth lay unconscious at the bottom.

The cold water splashed her face, immediately rousing her.

'Rats!' cried Jake. He sprinted down the moss-covered steps, which were slick with water. He lost his balance and tumbled the rest of the way.

Lorna ran in pursuit—but she had had the sense to download flight, and soared from the archway, hovering over the Great Wall.

Jake thumped down the steps—careering into Beth and knocking her flat again. He reached for the cloth but felt her arm around his neck, restraining him. The bundle was just out of reach.

Jake started to gurgle. 'Gah . . . you're killing . . . me . . .'

'That's . . . the idea!'

Jake realized he was choking because he was leaning forwards, like a dog on a lead. He suddenly switched direction. Beth wasn't prepared for the sudden lack of resistance. Jake reared backwards and butted her in the face.

Beth dropped, clutching her broken nose. Cartilage

cracked as her regeneration powers immediately kicked in, but it still hurt like mad.

Jake grabbed the cloth and pocketed it. Lorna swooped down by his side.

'Are you OK?'

Jake looked at her curiously. 'You lied. You said you didn't have any powers.'

Lorna sheepishly handed back his phone. Jake's eyes widened at the implication.

'Do you realize what you've done?'

'I'm not a Prime, I won't go crazy . . . but still, I had no choice, thanks to you. I guess that means I'm on your side now.'

Chameleon appeared in the watchtower arch they had just fled from—and a sudden clap of teleportation thunder from behind made them turn. Orsina was standing on the wall as it rose up and crested a hill. She smiled brightly at Jake.

'Hi, Jake. Miss me?'

Lorna's eyes narrowed like daggers. She glared at the newcomer; then turned her scowl on Jake. Her voice was ice cold.

'Who is *that*?'

'I don't have time to explain—'

Lorna's voice was dripping with jealousy. 'You better make time.'

Jake suddenly cottoned on to what she was thinking.

'You've got to be kidding me? Look . . . no . . . this . . . '

Orsina held her hand out and slightly wagged her fingers. 'I see you have two pendants there. Greedy boy. Forge'll take them.'

'What?' yelled Chameleon from the watchtower behind. 'We had a deal!'

'Sure. But it wasn't exclusive. First come first served, right? We're still working together against him . . . it's just that we'd like to have the pendants too.'

Jake stood at the bottom of the dipped wall, between the two feuding Supers. He was trapped. Glancing over the battlement revealed a long drop to the trees, and he only had levitation so he would float like a feather and be an easy target.

'How about one each?' Chameleon suggested. 'That way we can still honour our agreement?'

'That sounds fair.' Orsina casually skipped down the steps towards Jake and Lorna. Her gaze was now fixed on Lorna. There wasn't too much age difference between them.

'You must be Jake's little friend?' said Orsina with a condescending smile. 'He never mentioned you before.'

Lorna's temper snapped and she raised her hands in an attack stance. 'You horrible—'

'Temper, temper. As Jake will tell you, I'm pretty fast.'

As she drew close, Jake's energy whip suddenly snapped out and snagged around Orsina's legs, binding them together. The coil detached from his hand but remained firmly around her calves.

Jake shouldered past her, knocking her to the floor. 'I'm not chasing you again. Why don't you stay here and enjoy the view.' Orsina yelped, affronted. Jake ran up the steps, away from Chameleon, pulling Lorna behind him.

A fireball sailed across the wall—taking out a chunk of the battlement. Jake glanced behind to see Chameleon flying after them. He soared over Orsina, ignoring her pleas to be untied.

'Was she your girlfriend too?' enquired Lorna nastily.

'Lorn, you are really messed up in the head. You just dumped me!' Another explosion tore the steps from under their feet. Jake stumbled. Lorna stopped and wagged an accusing finger at him.

'That's not the point!'

'This isn't the time!'

Lorna's head snapped up to see Chameleon hurl another fireball. She raised her arm—a glowing shield forming in front of her. The fireball deflected like a ping-pong ball—shooting over the trees.

'And I've had enough of that too!' she shouted at Chameleon. She reached her other hand out as if she was swatting a fly in front of her face—and Chameleon felt a mighty telekinetic fist slam into him. The shape-changer spun through the air with a scream, crashing into the forest below.

Jake looked at her with new-found respect. 'That was awesome.'

Lorna had found Villain.net almost identical to Hero.com in layout—which was no surprise since the Council of Evil pirated the original. Although a lot of powers were different, the logic of the layout was the same and she had studied that long and hard with her brother.

They ran, cresting a peak in the hill. The next watch-tower lay a kilometre away; it was the only refuge they could take. Behind them, Orsina had managed to slacken her bonds. It was only a matter of time before she was free and she would easily catch them up with her super-speed.

'Did you download teleportation?' said Jake. His teleport power was still recharging in his body. For the moment it was useless, and Lorna's flight couldn't carry both of them so he didn't suggest it in case he reminded her that she could easily leave the battle.

'No. And I think I reached my download limit with four powers.'

Jake still had a residual benefit from his old powers. While others were limited to the number of powers they could download, in case they 'overloaded', Jake had managed to download half a dozen without any ill effect. However, that didn't help them right now.

They ran on—abruptly stopping again as the air ahead of them shimmered like water. It was an effect Jake and Lorna had never seen before.

A growling emanated from the shimmering portal. It sounded like a monstrous feral beast. Jake glanced behind to see that Orsina had freed herself, but hesitated as the portal appeared. Chameleon was scaling the wall halfway between Orsina and Jake, clearly not risking flying again while Lorna was around.

Members of Forge and the Hero Foundation blocked the path behind.

He turned back to the portal as a pair of Harley Davidson motorcycles prowled through it, a pair of mean-looking Hell's Angels riding them. They both wore shades and the leader had tattoos over both arms. Jake made out the words: EVIL on one, and ROCKS on the other.

They rolled to a halt a couple of metres away and the portal vanished like a mirage. The furthermost Hell's Angel raised his hand and blades sprang from his wrists forming a collar of spikes like an orbiting knuckle-duster. Small metal projectiles broke off and hovered over his hand, ready to fire on his command.

'Jake Hunter?' the lead Angel said in a raspy voice that sounded as if he had been smoking since birth.

China

Jake pointed a finger at Chameleon. 'There he is.'

The Angel's laugh was without humour. 'Right.' He spat a slimy string of chewing tobacco on the ground. 'You don't recognize me, do ya? I seen ya around the Council though. Word is spreadin' about what you're lookin' for. And I want in on the scam. In fact: I want it all.'

Jake looked around in disbelief. His enemies surrounded him, and they came from every camp. While the Angels made their dramatic entrance, Jake had skimmed through his phone. He found the power he was looking for—the icon was pretty self-explanatory.

'I don't think I'll be joining any of you guys at the moment. Thanks anyway.'

Chameleon and Orsina had edged forward, unsure what to make of the stand off.

'It wasn't an offer, Hunter. It was a demand.'

As he spoke, Jake glanced at the phone screen as it pulsed. He felt the new power flow through him.

'I don't do demands,' said Jake with a cocky smile. Then he jumped up, exactly as he had seen Seismic do in Los Angeles, and landed in a crouch—his fist power-driving into the wall.

The power Seismic had volunteered to Villain.net surged through Jake and into the wall. The entire wall shook as a violent earthquake struck it. Dust poured from between the bricks and the wall rippled in both directions like a sin wave with Jake and Lorna at the epicentre.

The Hell's Angels were closest and were thrown off their bikes. The wave thundered towards Chameleon and Orsina, knocking them both off their feet and disintegrating the battlements around them.

The earth tremor continued along the wall, collapsing the ancient watchtower Jake had fled from. The rubble kicked up a huge cloud of dust.

Jake grabbed Lorna's arm and sprang over the prone bikers. Metal darts shot from the silent Angel who was pinned under his heavy machine. Jake felt a cold stabbing pain in his leg—it felt as if he'd been shot.

He limped several metres before collapsing. Lorna tried to drag him to his feet.

'Come on!'

Jake gritted his teeth. His healing power was not as swift as it used to be. It pushed the metal darts slowly out of his thigh—but going out, they hurt almost as much as going in.

'Jake, don't make me leave you here!'

Jake tore the cloth bundle open and extracted the pendant—it looked exactly like all the others. He pulled the other from his pocket. His hands shook as he examined the symbols on the end. None of them matched. Jake's hands were trembling as he tried to push the two parts together.

China

'What are you doing?' Lorna glanced up to see Chameleon and Orsina try to make it past the Hell's Angels, but the biker villains were not ready to let them pass and a superpowered firefight was taking place.

CLICK. The two pendants linked together. They suddenly glowed with an internal light. Jake grinned, *something* was happening whether they were in the correct order or not. He reached into his other pocket and pulled out a small leather wallet and a coin-sized electronic disc stamped with the Foundation logo. He guessed it was a tracking device that Chameleon must have slipped in his pocket in the museum. Jake tossed it over the wall and opened the wallet—the other two pieces of the pendant lay inside.

'Four of them? You have four?' said Lorna.

'Yup. I thought carrying them myself would be the safest place.' It had been a good idea when he'd had his full powers; plus he didn't trust Leech at all so couldn't leave them in his safekeeping.

After some fumbling, Jake locked the two new pendants onto the others and the wand-assembly glowed blue. It was so bright in his hand he had to look away. He held the wand aloft, diverting his eyes. He knew the chances of placing them in the correct order was remote, but as long as they did *something* to get him out of this mess, he didn't care.

Chameleon, Orsina, and the Angels stopped fighting as they were washed with brilliant light. Chameleon snapped back into his human form, his face a mask of horror.

'No . . . how? No . . . Jake! Don't do it! You don't know the right combination!'

Jake felt the Core Power rush through his body. Every nerve tingled and he felt suddenly powerful; unstoppable. Even though he still lacked two parts of the pendant for full mastery, it felt as if the universe was at his fingertips.

A pulse of energy shot to the sky, forming a solid column of light. The fog began to swirl around the beam.

Lorna's long hair started to rise. Loose leaves and debris drifted skywards. The entire forest creaked as tree branches were tugged upwards by an invisible force.

Jake suddenly knew what Core Power he had in his hands. A power that shaped galaxies, formed stars, destroyed planets, and turned the universe.

He had the power of gravity.

The sky suddenly split asunder as atom-sized gravitons clashed, forming a swirling black hole over the Great Wall of China that swelled in size, almost a quarter of a mile across.

Gravity immediately went crazy as the black hole vacuumed the fog in a second—then the air became clouded as a billion pieces of detritus were pulled upwards.

Jake was unaffected, but Lorna had to hold on to him tightly as her legs were yanked upwards. She was upside down as she clung on to his jacket.

The gravity field intensified. Boulders, and bricks from the wall, were inexorably sucked upwards—the Great Wall was disassembling a brick at a time.

With nothing to hold on to, Chameleon, Orsina, the Angels and their bikes drifted up.

Jake felt a thrill of power he'd never experienced before as he unleashed one of the most destructive forces in the universe . . .

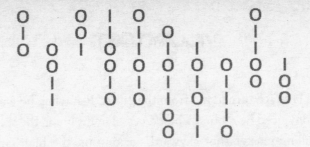

Collision Course

An uprooted tree shot past Jake; the branches and trailing roots whipped at him, breaking his concentration. He suddenly took stock of the whirlwind around him.

The black hole above resembled a swirling galaxy. Everything around him was being slowly pulled upwards; the air was choked with debris that was falling up at the same pace it would drop to earth.

The Great Wall itself was drawn into the sky as if it was nothing more than a ribbon, with only the section Jake was standing on remaining grounded. Some sections crumbled apart, others remained intact but rose, still attached to the huge chunks of bedrock they were built on.

Jake came to his senses and yanked the pendant down, mentally commanding the black hole away. At first, nothing happened. Jake began to doubt if he had any control over the destructive force. He tried harder, willing with every fibre that the black hole simply *go away*.

His face turned red from the effort. Just when he was convinced he'd burst a blood vessel in his brain, the spi-ralling cluster shot skyward, sucking up the high cir-rocumulus clouds as it vanished through the upper reaches of the atmosphere. Without its mighty pull of gravity everything fell from the sky.

Lorna collapsed at Jake's feet. Stones, twigs, insects, and soil rained down on them. Lorna raised her shield to protect them both.

For miles in either direction, the Great Wall slammed back to earth in piles of rubble. Only two watchtowers didn't break apart on impact.

The two Hell's Angels had been consumed by the black hole, but Chameleon, Orsina, and Beth had bet-ter luck and crashed back to the ground amongst piles of dirt and felled trees.

An eerie silence fell across the countryside.

With shaking hands, Jake disconnected the pendants and stashed them in his pocket. His fingers sank into Lorna's arm.

'I think it's time to go,' he whispered.

His teleportation powers were fully charged, and whisked them away from the mass destruction before the last pebble had dropped.

Bryce Campbell frowned as he stared at his monitor

screen. Something was not right. He adjusted the range on his instruments. The readings were the same.

He stared thoughtfully through the soundproof glass at the rest of the control room beyond. Dozens of Air Force technicians sat at desks, carefully scrutinizing their screens, each one of them monitoring a section of airspace across the US continent. Giant monitors showed air traffic in different parts of the world.

Bryce glanced back to his own screen. What he was looking at didn't make sense. He scooped up a telephone and spoke his concerns to the general who supervised the North American Aerospace Defense Command, commonly known as NORAD.

Built under the Cheyenne Mountain in Colorado, NORAD was approachable by a single tunnel carved into the rock, which ended in a nuclear blast-proof door. NORAD constantly monitored the skies for potential threats. Campbell's desk monitored outer space, tracking any potential meteor strikes and the thousands of tons of space junk and satellites in orbit around the earth.

Moments later, a lean aging general entered the room. 'My shift finishes in one hour, I hope you ain't brought me anything that's gonna upset the barbecue I got planned? Those jokers out there are telling me there's some kinda power blackout happening here and in Europe.'

Campbell always felt nervous around the general. 'I . . . I'm not sure, sir. It's nothing to do with the black-out. Our sensors picked up something unusual in the atmosphere. Look.'

He tapped a screen that tracked every piece of space junk—from dropped spanners to secret satellites. There was a large hole in the band of junk.

'Where'd it all go?' asked the general.

'One minute they were there, the next . . .'

'Are we talking about some kind of space weaponry?' The general's darkest fear was that another country would build satellites capable of shooting down their own.

'No, sir. The empty patch on the screen is about the size of Australia.'

'A meteor then?'

'If something that big had struck, then we wouldn't be having this conversation. We'd be extinct.'

The general impatiently slapped both palms against the desk. 'I don't believe some scrapyard went up there and recycled it all, so give me an answer!'

'I pulled the range of the sensors back, using the lunar base.' While the public believed that moon missions had ended in the seventies, the military had been building an array of sensors on the lunar surface to monitor the earth. It offered the perfect platform to peer back at the planet. 'And I found this.'

Collision Course

The general stared at the live video feed. It was black.

'OK . . . ?'

'You should be able to see the earth,' Campbell prompted. 'Something's blocking the view.'

'Maybe the camera's broken?'

'Diagnostics work fine. I pulled up different wave spectrums and saw nothing.' The general still looked blank. Campbell suppressed his sigh. 'Something is sucking up all the light and all the radiation . . . it's a black hole, sir.'

The general was dumbstruck.

Campbell was giddy now he had the general's attention and could show off his skills. He spoke rapidly as he typed.

'So I tapped into the network of gravity sensors across the planet and in orbit using the GRACE satellites and mapped out any fluctuations in the field. And there the data correlated to a singularity . . .' He noticed the general's blank expression. 'Er . . . that is to say, the Newtons measured . . . Look, it doesn't matter. My point is I backtracked the data and discovered it was created here. On Earth I mean, not Colorado . . . but I know where it originated. China.'

The general's mouth hung open. 'Is this some kind of new super-weapon?'

Campbell let him dwell on that news for a moment, before adding the bad part.

'And it's growing bigger.'

The general grabbed the phone and stabbed an internal line. 'Get me through to Special Operations. I need the Enforcers!'

Campbell tugged at the general's sleeve; he had just noticed something else. 'General . . . you need to take a look at this. *This* is really bad . . .'

When Jake and Lorna appeared, Jake immediately cringed, expecting another punch from Lorna . . . but it didn't happen. She was too busy shivering from the intense cold.

'Where are we?' she said through numb lips.

Jake rubbed his still-black eye as he glanced around. 'Tibet. Stay close.' With trembling hands he accessed a power he always used when he arrived. The phone's cache held small quantities of whatever powers had been recently downloaded. It was like a browser history, and useful if the user was ever away from a phone signal.

The warming power eased away the cold. Jake put his arm around Lorna to share it. He felt uncomfortable doing it, but Lorna didn't seem to mind. She looked around their new location without much interest. She had been through too many bizarre situations to be surprised any more. 'Tibet, huh? Is this your new home away from home when you want to avoid me?'

Jake ignored her, and marched silently to the main doors. As ever, the monk opened them as they approached and led them inside. He bowed as the door silently closed.

'He is expecting you.'

Lorna caught the flicker of distrust on Jake's face. 'Really? I hadn't even known I was coming until a few minutes ago.'

Jake followed the monk, but stopped when he noticed Lorna wasn't following.

'What's the matter?'

Lorna pouted. After everything he had put her through, she was damned if she was going to follow him again.

'You've made me an outcast, Jake. You've turned me against the Foundation; you made me attack Chameleon while you had your own people, the Foundation and Forge chasing after you! I stood by you as you used some illegal power and opened up a black hole, destroying a World Heritage site! And on top of that ... that ... that girl ... ' She was fuming too much to continue.

Jake didn't know what to say. *'Shut up'*, or *'You're obviously dumb to get everything so mixed up'*, didn't seem the right thing. Instead, Jake did something equally bad. He nodded to the monk.

'They can access Hero.com, or V-net, whatever you prefer. Download something and teleport yourself out then.' He left the room, suddenly realizing that the sentence he had planned to sound neutral and helpful, in fact sounded cold and callous. He turned round to correct himself, but the door closed with a deep bass thump.

'Jake Hunter,' echoed Leech's voice from across the new, smaller chamber. 'You never fail to please. How was it? How was your first encounter with unlimited power?'

'So you know what I did?'

Leech chuckled. 'Don't forget,' he pointed to his eyes, 'I see far and wide.'

'It was . . . incredible. Scary too . . . but gravity? So I can make things fall up and stuff? Not exactly earth shattering power.'

Leech laughed loudly. 'Earth shattering is exactly what it is. Didn't you study physics at school?'

Jake shrugged. He'd hated physics lessons, as he never saw how they'd be useful in real life. Who would have thought they'd help him rule the world or destroy the bastions of good and evil?

'Gravity keeps us on the planet. Without it we would spin off into space. Not that that would matter because the earth's atmosphere would be torn away and the planet would be a barren rock. Gravity holds galaxies together; ensures planets revolve around suns and binds the entire universe together! It can pull tower blocks to the ground.' He pulled a book from his desk and let it drop to the floor. The dull thud made Jake jump. 'Or even just this book or feather . . . yet this incredible force that can drag planets into the sun can be defeated very easily.' He jumped on the spot and smiled. 'See? Even an old man can beat gravity . . . if only for a short while.'

'OK, I get it's powerful. I saw what damage the four parts of it did. I think that's enough to beat the Council and Foundation. I don't need the other two pieces.'

'But you do, Jake. Without the last two parts you won't have full mastery.'

'I don't need it.'

Leech sneered, his usually affable expression looked dark. 'That's typical of you kids! You think because you know a little about something that you know it all. For a start, you placed the pendants together haphazardly. You paid no heed to the markings.'

'But it still worked.'

'No. You created something you had no real control over! The symbols on the pendants are precise mathematical equations designed to limit the power! Placing them together as you did is akin to mixing every chemical you can lay your hands on and hoping it doesn't blow up in your face!' Leech was shouting now. Jake wasn't happy being berated. He also noticed that Leech looked less wrinkled and much more energetic than last time they met. 'That's why we needed the processor. Even now Forge is close to deciphering the equations because they exercised patience! Where did that black hole you created go to?'

'I just got rid of it.'

'No you didn't. You just cast it away into space.'

'So?'

Leech clenched his fists. 'So if you had full mastery you could have vanquished it as easily as you had made it. Instead it is now lurking just beyond the earth's orbit. The gravitational pull has affected the moon's orbit.'

Despite Leech's haranguing, Jake was feeling tired, lulled by the monastery's calming incense and relaxing atmosphere. 'It's the moon. Big deal.'

Leech's eyes narrowed. 'Jake, you *need* the last two pieces for two reasons. One, you promised me you'd kill Kirby. Two, your black hole has pulled the moon from its orbit. It's now on a collision course to Earth.'

Absolute silence. With no air in space, sound couldn't travel. Sunlight glinted off the giant solar panels that formed the bulk of the International Space Station. The tiny modules that provided the living spaces for the crew of six looked fragile against the blue marble of earth below it.

Inside, the multinational crew could drift and spin in a state of almost zero-g, commonly called microgravity. Right now, the team were at panic stations as they received a stream of data from NORAD. Their own instruments confirmed that a black hole had mysteriously appeared and that it had dragged the moon out of orbit.

Their frantic analysis was suddenly interrupted by a dull thump that shook the ISS, and a pressure wave that made their ears pop. The common fear was that a breach in the hull would depressurize the station, blast their oxygen into space, killing them all in the frigid void beyond.

'It came from Cupola,' said a Russian cosmonaut, examining the environmental readout. 'Pressure is stable. It isn't a hull breach.'

'What is it?' asked the American commander.

Commander Mather had had his share of adventure when supervillains had hijacked a private shuttle he had been piloting. He had been forced to eject from the shuttle, leaving it, and the villains, to crash-land on Earth. The experience had shaken Mather, and he had been looking forward to a relaxing mission on the ISS.

Nobody seemed keen to investigate. Commander Mather sighed, and drifted from *Zvezda* service module.

'I guess I'll check it out.'

The Cupola was on the other side of the station. He drifted through two other modules before realizing that nobody had followed him. A com-set hooked round his ear kept him in touch with the rest of his team.

Something clanged in the module ahead. Everything on the station was tethered as any free-floating object was a hazard.

'I hear something ahead,' he reported.

'Be careful,' came the reply.

Mather could hear more scraping. He couldn't shake the feeling somebody else was close by—impossible though that was.

He edged forward into the Unity module and held his breath—was it possible that somebody was inside the Cupola? It was an observation platform that allowed the crew a splendid view of Earth, and at times, the moon.

Commander Mather felt his heart hammering in his chest. He saw a shadow moving against the curved wall of the pod, verifying his suspicions.

He slowly reached out and unfastened a steel wrench from a Velcro utility pouch on the wall. Logically, he

Collision Course

knew nobody else could be aboard, but his run-in with the superpowered freaks had defied logic.

'Hey!' He shouted as a distraction—the wrench was already arcing towards the back of the figure's head.

Jake Hunter felt the pang of cold steel hitting his skull and he head-butted the reinforced observation dome.

'OW!' He spun round and glared at Commander Mather. 'What's wrong with you? Do you always hit people on the back of the head?'

The shock of seeing a teenage boy dressed in a grubby T-shirt and equally unwashed jeans lasted for only a second. He remembered the two young boys who had been fighting on the nosecone of his shuttle when it had taken off.

'You're one of them!' he said accusingly.

'Huh?'

'You can . . . fly . . . and things . . . '

'The word you are looking for is: superpowered. Yes. I'm one of them.' He rubbed the back of his head. Already the bump was beginning to heal, and his teleportation power was slowly recharging, but it was not yet ready to use. He was feeling queasy from the weightless environment: it was like the feeling he got when his dad drove very quickly over a hill and his stomach lurched . . . except it never fell back down.

'Look, I don't want any trouble. I need help.'

'Help? Do you realize where you are?'

'On the ISS I hope. I needed somewhere to go up here. Somewhere I could see if it's true.'

'You know about the black hole?'

Jake avoided looking him in the eye. 'Mmm, yeah. That. I was talking about the moon. It doesn't look like it's moving . . . '

They both stared through the Cupola bubble. The moon was no larger than a coin.

'It is. Two hours ago it was 365, 578 kilometres away. It moves closer or further away from the earth because of its orbit. Ten minutes ago it was 312, 241 clicks. That's beyond the moon's *perigee*, uh, the closest it ever gets to Earth.'

Jake felt his stomach knot. This man didn't know him, therefore didn't have any reason to lie to him. 'What does that mean?'

'At the rate of acceleration, it will hit the planet in about a day. If it does, the world will crack open like an egg and every single thing on it will be extinct.'

Jake's tongue felt numb. What could he say to that? He had just set in motion the extinction of all life on Earth. He had only wanted to strike out at his enemies, and look where that had got him. He licked his dry lips.

'Could the earth get sucked in too? Can it be stopped?'

Collision Course

'The earth has a heavier mass. Eventually it would be affected, but that would be after the collision. By then it will just be a floating group of shattered rock. We could fire every single nuclear missile on the planet at the moon, but it won't do much. Besides, the Pentagon has an orbital missile fleet up here—strictly top secret, but since we're all going to die in twenty-four hours, I don't mind telling you. They shot some high-intensity lasers at the moon, but the light bent—'

'You can't bend lasers.' That was something Jake was sure about.

'Black holes can. Even light can't escape their gravity. And that's what's caused the moon to de-orbit. A black hole just appeared from nowhere. The hole itself is slowly moving in an elliptical orbit. Half an hour ago it was blocking sight of the moon, now it has moved around slightly so we can all see our impending doom. Our only hope is that the black hole will suck up the moon or at least divert it, like water sloshing around a drain. But according to my calculations, that's unlikely.'

'Twenty-four hours?'

'That's an estimate. It could change. It could be sooner.'

The sound of hailstones suddenly reverberated through the ISS. Mather looked around in alarm, and activated his headset.

'What is it?'

A stressed French voice spoke so loudly, Jake could hear it. 'Meteor shower!'

'Oh no . . .'

Jake was puzzled, he'd seen shooting stars from his garden on Earth and remembered his sister telling him that they were meteorites burning up in the atmosphere. 'How bad can that be?'

'The black hole is affecting the entire region. It's pulling any bits of junk floating through space and diverting them straight towards us!'

The clattering increased as tiny meteorites, some no bigger than a grain of sand, struck the space station. The shimmying grew worse—and an alarm suddenly sounded. Seconds later a pressurized pipe in the module next to them broke, sending a stream of compressed gas into the confined space.

Jake glanced out of the observation dome in time to see a rock, the size of a football, sail past and smash into one of the giant solar panel arrays.

The delicate panels smashed into millions of fragments that spun in every direction. The twisted groan of steel reverberated through the space station as the solar panel gantry was torn away.

The interior lights suddenly went off; only a handful of emergency lights remained.

'We're on emergency power!' screamed Mather. 'Everybody, get ready to abandon ship!' He grabbed

Collision Course

Jake's arm. 'Come with me, kid. There's a Soyuz craft docked on the other end of the station. We can leave in that.'

Jake didn't waste time arguing. He couldn't teleport out until his power had recharged. He drifted after Commander Mather, down the length of the module, when something the size of a golf ball suddenly punctured the fragile wall of the section ahead—and out of the wall opposite. The effect was instantaneous.

Jake heard a roaring noise as all the air in the ISS rushed towards the hull breach. He bounced into the commander as they were sucked towards the breach on a hurricane force wave of air. The cabin around them was suddenly filled with anything that wasn't bolted down. A video camera ricocheted from Jake's head.

One second later the pressure door between them and the module ahead suddenly slammed shut—and Jake and Commander Mather careered into it. The pressure door had just saved them from being jettisoned into space.

'Alpha!' yelled Mather into his mic. 'Come in!'

'Commander, you're alive!' came a relieved voice. 'We made it into the Soyuz. Where are you?'

'On the other side.' There was no sense of drama in the commander's voice, just the acceptance that he couldn't leave with them. 'Eject.'

'Sir—!'

The entire station shook again as meteors took out more solar panels. Jake glanced through a small viewing port and saw the earth spiral dizzyingly out of view— they had been knocked out of orbit.

'Go!' shouted Mather.

They both felt the clunk reverberate through the space station as the escape pod jettisoned from the structure. Through the small portal they watched their chance of freedom drift away.

'Can you magic us out of here?' Mather asked, still gazing through the window.

'Not right now.'

'One more hit and we're dead. Not that it matters. There's not much oxygen left in this module. Most of it vented outside.'

The station shuddered again as fuel tanks were pierced, streams of liquid jetting out.

The commander suddenly spotted something drifting in the module, knocked loose by the impact. It was an EVA spacesuit. He kicked himself from the wall and intercepted it. The look of hope was dashed when he realized there was only one.

'Here. You put this on. It might buy you some time.'

Jake was speechless. For the first time in his life, he was being offered something for purely unselfish reasons.

'Don't you have a family?' asked Jake.

Collision Course

'Wife and two kids; three and five.' His firm expression quivered slightly as he thought about them. 'I knew the risks coming up here. Put this on.'

Jake was rocked. He was looking at a true, selfless hero. And he didn't possess *any* superpowers. Jake felt a coward as his instinct was to accept the offered spacesuit. He glanced out of the portal—it was better than looking at somebody who was making him feel incredibly guilty.

The manoeuvring boosters on the side of the Soyuz escape pod looked like small camera flashes as the pod positioned itself for re-entry into the atmosphere. What nobody could see from inside the pod was that they were positioning themselves for Earth re-entry right in the path of a huge meteor, the size of a car.

'Oh my God . . .'

Commander Mather followed his gaze and gasped in anguish.

'Radio them! Tell them to move!' said Jake.

'I can't, the external communication antenna was ripped off! I can't reach them out there!'

The five astronauts were about to die because of events Jake had set in motion. He'd done a lot of bad things in his time, and he was starting to regret his selfish actions. He hated feeling this way, but Commander Mather had stirred a moral compass in his head he didn't know he possessed.

10110100010000011001010011001001101

He slid his phone out. Typical, he was probably flying right past the telecom satellite and he still couldn't get a signal! And now his ability to manifest powers at will had faded, he felt useless . . .

Then he remembered the raw power reserve built into the phone, designed for exactly the moment he had no signal. He had an idea. It was wild, but it might just work.

He activated the powers and felt them kick into his body.

'Put on the suit. I'm going out there to save them.'

'What? How?'

Jake didn't have time to answer. He triggered the shield Lorna had downloaded from his phone. She had only formed a small shield over her arm, but Jake concentrated hard—forming a complete bubble around him. Then he apported, appearing in between the Soyuz and the meteor.

The incredulous faces of the astronauts peered from the single porthole at the boy in casual clothes, surrounded by a bubble that was only visible against the inky blackness when debris bounced off it, causing it to spark blue.

Jake fought the massive jolt of vertigo that swept over him as he gazed at the earth from two hundred and twenty miles up. He broke out in a cold sweat and focused on the lumbering meteor. His hands glowed bright green and he unleashed a stream of radioactive plasma.

The meteor instantly exploded. Jake whooped at the ease with which he had averted disaster . . . until he saw that he had simply broken the meteor up into hundreds of smaller fragments that still headed towards the fragile capsule.

Jake fired again and again—doing nothing more than break down the chunks and create even more projectiles that would shred the Soyuz apart.

'C'mon, Jake,' he encouraged himself. 'Think!'

Stopping the meteor was impossible . . . and he only had about thirty seconds left . . .

Then the obvious conclusion struck him. He zoomed over to the escape pod, thankful that his levitation powers worked just like flying when there was no fixed up or down to hamper them. He wrung his hands, as if cleaning off the radioactive power, and initiated another power Lorna had used as a non-lethal alternative on Chameleon.

He placed his hands against the cold metal of the capsule and let the water jets pour from his hands. He'd never bothered to listen to his physics teacher drone on about Newton's laws of motion—and was surprised to find himself propelled away from the larger mass of the capsule. He countered that by flying towards the ship, while still firing the jets of water.

The Soyuz began to inch forward, but it was painfully slow. Meteor grains started to fizzle against Jake's shield, heralding the arrival of the larger devastating chunks.

He pushed harder, the exertion causing him to sweat and feel faint. He wondered how much air was trapped in the bubble with him? Probably not enough.

The escape pod rapidly picked up speed—drifting out of the path of the meteors. Jake's shield exploded with a fury of impacts as he was struck. A sixth-sense warned him that the shield-power would expire at any moment, leaving him stranded in space. He apported back into the ISS module—

—just as his shield fizzled away! He felt exhausted and slumped, but rather than drop to his knees, he lazily spun around the pod.

'That was incredible!' Commander Mather's voice was muffled from beneath the closed helmet. He had the spacesuit sealed, ready for the inevitable.

They both saw the Soyuz's boosters fire as it rotated into position for re-entry.

'Will they be OK?' asked Jake with concern.

'If the heat shield wasn't damaged, and it looked fine to me, they'll be fine. That was a brave and incredible thing you did.'

Jake didn't know how to respond to the rare compliment; so he didn't.

Collision Course

'But I guess this is it for us,' added Mather ominously.

Jake gritted his teeth. He felt a surge of determination wash through him. He couldn't die now, that would leave the planet helpless. Admittedly, helpless from a threat he had created, but that wasn't the point.

Jake gripped the Commander's spacesuit with both hands. 'I don't think so.'

The entire space station suddenly ripped open behind them and everything was sucked into space. Jake held his breath as he was dragged out at a phenomenal speed.

A second later his body responded to the ice cold of space and he saw his skin turn pale as it iced up. Paradoxically his arms felt incredibly hot as his blood started to boil. None of that mattered because his eyeballs were starting to freeze . . .

That all started to happen within the first second. A millisecond later Jake sensed his teleport power had fully recharged and wasted no time in activating it. He and Commander Mather suddenly vanished . . .

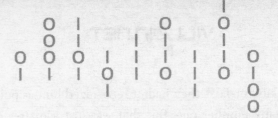

Restoration

The cup of tea tasted wonderful. Jake closed his eyes and relaxed, feeling that he could go to sleep instantly.

He recalled how he had teleported with Commander Mather to the middle of the lawn at the back of the White House in Washington DC. Since the commander was American and Jake didn't know from exactly where, he had brought to mind the most iconic American image he could think of. He had dismissed the Statue of Liberty, because he had already destroyed that and didn't think it would go down well if he returned to the scene of the crime.

Commander Mather had had tears of gratitude in his eyes when he'd finally taken off the space helmet. Jake had felt elated. He didn't know if it was from exposure to outer space, or if that was what it felt like to be a hero.

The moment was interrupted by a squad of heavily armed Secret Service men thundering across the lawn to arrest the teenager and joker in a spacesuit who had just broken into the grounds of one of the most heavily guarded homes in the world.

Luckily for Jake, they hadn't recognized him as public enemy number one. But that was just a matter of time. As he lay spreadeagled on the ground he winked at Commander Mather, then apported several metres out of the White House gardens.

For the next thirty minutes Jake had played cat and mouse with the Secret Service and police who were combing the area for him. He didn't need the hassle of a manhunt as he was starting to feel tired and ill. He waited for his teleportation to recharge . . . but it didn't. It had expired—something that had never happened to him before. Jake was furious because of the time he had wasted. Luckily, his phone was still working and had a signal so he could access Villain.net.

After all the danger he had been through, and with the annihilation threat approaching, there was only one place he wanted to be.

He quantum tunnelled home.

'Like your tea?' asked his mum.

Jake forced his eyes open, relieved to be back in his old house, with parents who no longer suffered amnesia about who he was.

'It's great, Mum.'

'Hungry? It's nearly dinner time.'

Jake's stomach automatically rumbled at the mention of dinner.

Restoration

'These power blackouts are getting worse,' said Jake's dad. 'I haven't seen anything like it before.'

Jake noticed a look of concern cross his mother's face. 'I hope Beth is all right. Who'd have thought she would be the one to go off the rails and become a wild child?'

'My money was always on him,' said his dad with a smile.

Jake had wondered what Eric Kirby had said to his parents when they woke up in a Foundation hospital to see everybody was chasing him, and Beth was claiming that she didn't know who he was. But his parents appeared to buy into the cover story that they had both been assigned to specialist schools for behavioural problems. Jake didn't push the issue.

'Which leads us onto a serious matter, Jake,' said his dad with the tone Jake knew spelt trouble.

'What is it?'

'We haven't seen much of you since you were, um, transferred to that boarding school. However, we've received a letter from them. It seems that you haven't been to lessons for a week!'

'You've been bunking, haven't you?' said his mum.

Jake used all his willpower to stop the incriminating smile inch across his cheeks, but couldn't. This was obviously some red herring Eric Kirby had thrown in to the situation to annoy Jake. Because the Foundation

was using Beth, they had deemed the house to be a neutral location. Jake suspected the Foundation or Enforcers were watching him, but they had never made a move to apprehend him. These pranks were the only way Kirby could provoke him here; it wasn't the first time they'd received letters from his phantom headmaster. The world was in peril, the moon was about to obliterate everything, and his parents were worried about him missing school that didn't even exist!

'It's not a laughing matter,' scolded his dad. 'We've been very relaxed with you in the past, maybe too liberal, but this isn't acceptable.'

Jake forced himself to look chagrined. 'Sorry. I've been busy . . . '

He saw his parents look uncomfortable. What did they know?

The doorbell rang, breaking the awkward atmosphere. Jake slammed the mug onto the table, spilling the tea, and leapt to his feet, instantly alert.

'I'll get it,' his dad said.

'Jake! You'll stain the carpet! Go and get a cloth!'

As much as Jake loved his parents and was relieved to have them back, he still couldn't spend any length of time with them without getting irritated.

He knew the Enforcers monitored the house: they were a United Nations-run team of soldiers, who

Restoration

operated without superpowers, keeping those who had any in check. However, he was certain that they still couldn't detect when he quantum tunnelled in. He was certain that the Hero Foundation had the house under surveillance, maybe even had bugs and cameras inside—but they had never attacked. Perhaps Kirby didn't want to alienate Beth by sending soldiers into her house? But with the world on the brink of destruction he guessed that such a truce wouldn't hold.

'It's for you, Jake,' drifted his dad's voice from the hallway.

Jake nervously thumbed his phone in his pocket. In his haste, he had only downloaded the one power to escape, and everything else had expired.

He peeked into the hallway. His father was blocking the view of the visitor.

It had to be a trap. He nervously positioned himself at the bottom of the stairs. At the first hint of trouble he would bound up them and tunnel away.

His father called again. 'Jake?'

This time he moved just enough to reveal the visitor—it was Lorna.

'Right here, Dad.'

His dad looked between them both with an idiotic grin, waiting for the introduction. When none was forthcoming he nodded, 'Right-o,' and made a quick departure into the living room, winking knowingly at

Jake. Jake felt his cheeks blush—how come parents could always find a way to embarrass you?

'What are you doing here?' he said suspiciously.

'Oh thanks. That's very nice of you.'

'I'm sorry . . . I just had a very bad . . . day. Sorry,' muttered Jake.

Lorna's eyes narrowed. 'For what?'

'For . . . what I said back in Tibet, leaving you behind . . . missing your birthday. I didn't mean any of it. Don't take this the wrong way, but how did you know I was here?'

'I have my sources,' she said mysteriously. 'Actually, I was just passing and thought I'd call by, see if you were around. You mentioned you come home every now and again.'

'I'm not staying for long.'

'I didn't think so. I want to come with you.'

Jake looked at her curiously. 'Why? I thought we'd split?'

Lorna hesitated, and Jake thought she looked surprised by his comment. Then she shrugged. 'Um . . . because we make a good team.'

She seemed to be in much better spirits, which Jake was happy about. The less emotional baggage they had the better.

Jake thought for a moment. 'Sure. I have to get back to Leech. I left in a hurry.'

Restoration

Then they were suddenly plunged into darkness. Every streetlight went, and all the houses were nestled in blackness. A chorus of barking dogs started up.

'My dad said this has been happening a lot,' said Jake, wondering if it was something he had accidentally triggered.

'Look at the sky,' he said in awe.

Without light pollution, they could see every star. Their eyes quickly adjusted to take in the white smear of the milky way. Even though he had almost died in space, it was still an awe-inspiring sight.

'Incredible, isn't it?' muttered Lorna. 'Look at the moon. It looks huge.'

Jake followed her finger. The moon was low in the sky, and it looked bigger and clearer than ever.

'Mmm,' said Jake. 'About that . . . ' He didn't know how to break the news to her. 'Let's go. I have a lot of stuff to do.'

He shouted into the house, saying goodbye to his parents. He didn't have time to get into a discussion with them, so slammed the front door closed.

'Jake?' His dad ran out of the house in time to see a flurry of snow fall onto the driveway. He thought it was odd as there wasn't a cloud in the sky and it was a rather warm night.

He also had the strangest feeling he wouldn't see his son again.

* * *

Jake and Lorna shivered. Once again they had been ill-prepared for the snowstorm outside the monastery. A monk had been waiting with hot green tea for them inside. Then they were led to a large hall Jake had never seen before. He was beginning to suspect that Leech was far more than the monk's guest. The old man looked more full of energy than Jake. The Tibetan lifestyle was treating him well.

The room housed a huge orrery. Mechanical arms extended from an orb suspended midway to the ceiling, holding dozens of other objects: planets, moons, and comets. They all spun round on a complex array of gears that moved them in relevant orbit around the central sun, while each planet rotated on its axis, and their individual moons around them. It was an intricate, delicate machine.

The grinding of gears was as loud as a factory floor. Leech had his back to them, watching the celestial ballet. He spoke without turning round.

'Fascinating, isn't it?'

'It's beautiful,' said Lorna.

Jake was nonchalant. 'It's OK. Shouldn't we be more worried about doing something to stop what's happening.'

Leech's shoulders sagged, and he turned around.

Restoration

'You know what you need to do. The last two pieces are all that's stopping you. The damage caused by the moon's proximity is already echoing around the world.'

Jake glanced at Lorna. He had briefed her when they were trudging through the snow towards the monastery. She knew the moon was on a collision course, although Jake didn't see the point in telling her where the last two pendants were.

'I never heard anything about it,' said Lorna.

'That's because half the world is experiencing major power outages due to some crazy supervillain on the loose. But everybody is suffering.' Leech indicated to the model Earth with the moon orbiting in its right and proper place. 'The moon's gravity helps create the tides. But it is no longer orbiting the earth as it should. With the increased and constant gravitational pull, there are no tides. Weather systems are reacting to this, and major super-storms are already brewing, pounding coastal cities and causing flooding and devastation all over the world, and it will only get worse as the moon draws nearer. Get the pendants from Kirby and Necros and you can stop this. Kill them, and you can save the world.'

Jake heard Lorna gasp. 'Kill Eric Kirby? Jake, you never mentioned this.'

'Lorna . . .'

'I can't let you do that.'

There were tears in her eyes. Jake was puzzled; he could understand her anguish at the thought of killing Kirby, but he had caused Lorna no end of trouble, so why was she so emotional?

'We haven't got time to discuss this,' said Jake calmly.

'Don't say that, Jake. Tell me that's not your plan?'

'He has the pendant. He's not just going to give it to me.'

Lorna brushed aside the tears with her sleeve. She was suddenly calm. 'Last time, the Foundation used me to get at you, and I swore I'd never do it again.'

Jake's eyes narrowed. 'That's how you knew I was at home. The Foundation told you?'

'No, Jake.' She slid a mobile from her pocket.

Jake saw the distinct Forge logo on the screen—he was stunned. 'No . . . '

Lorna breathed sharply as she spoke into her phone. 'You have the coordinates? He's here.'

Jake scowled and raised his hand to blow the phone apart—suddenly remembering that the quantum tunnel was the only power he had downloaded and that had expired in his constantly altering body. He knew he must investigate the side effects he'd been suffering from the EMP pulse that had engulfed him in Iraq, but he didn't have time.

'What have you done?' he hissed. He hoped Leech

Restoration

would intervene at any moment, but the old man had vanished. *Probably hiding, like all Primes,* thought Jake bitterly. They thought they were more valuable than Downloaders because they had been born with their powers.

An amber light blazed from Lorna's finger and Jake found himself paralysed. With a loud bang, Pete suddenly appeared in the room. He looked delighted to see Jake was incapacitated.

'Hunter, great to see you, mate.' He coughed, spitting blood from his mouth. He reached into Jake's pockets and retrieved the four pendants. 'Wow . . . they . . . they don't look like much, do they? I was expecting something pretty impressive like the thing Lord Eon had me chasing around for. You know, somebody should think of a better way of disposing things rather than leaving them lying around all over the place. But this has saved me a whole heap of trouble. Thanks.'

Jake wanted to scream and shout. He wanted to shoot Pete in the face and scream at Lorna for being a traitor. Didn't she understand that he was trying to *save* the world? Couldn't she see that Pete and Chameleon were working together for their own selfish reasons?

Pete slapped Jake on the arm. Since he was rigid, he rocked like a statue.

'Word on the grapevine is that you're losing your powers, mate. I was going to ask you to stop this virus you put in me, but . . . I guess that's too late now. Chameleon reckons he can use this Core Power to reverse the effects. I have my doubts, I mean, it's gravity, right? But he says Core Powers are at the heart of all superpowers. Maybe the gravity will drag your little virus out of me? Who knows how it all works? Fingers crossed anyway, eh? At least, if this is it for me, you will be dead before I am. We let the Enforcers know where you are. They've called an air strike in on this place. In a couple of minutes it will be rubble and you will be history.'

The door behind them suddenly slammed open—twelve angry looking monks in bright yellow and orange robes stood beyond, all standing in a martial arts stance.

'Aw, give me a break,' said Pete. 'Kung-fu monks?'

'Attack!' roared Leech. Pete and Lorna saw the old man appear from the dark shadows. They had both been so focused on Jake, and assumed that the ex-hero was no longer a threat, that they hadn't noticed him slip away.

The monks charged forward with a battle cry.

Several cartwheeled through the doorway, others somersaulted over their colleagues while the rear flank charged with a roar. It was a rapid, coordinated attack.

Three monks kicked Pete in rapid succession, tossing him across the room into a display of astrolabes.

The monks were just as violent to Lorna. One swept

Restoration

her feet away as another chopped her across the shoulder—sending her reeling across the floor.

Pete was overwhelmed with grogginess as the brass instruments clattered around him. His body swelled as it absorbed energy from the multiple impacts. Before he knew it, four monks were on top of him, trying to prise the pendants from his fist.

Three monks advanced on Lorna. She opened her jaw, hyperextended like a snake's, as she screamed a sonic wail that distorted the air, plucking the monks off their feet. One smashed into the large bronze mass of Neptune as it swept about the orrery. The other two spun back through the doorway.

Jake could only watch helplessly as the fight escalated around him. The paralysing power Lorna had administered would last several minutes more. His eyes were starting to feel dry and sore, and he desperately wanted to blink and rub them, but even his eyelids wouldn't move.

A monk landed in front of him. Jake recognized him as the monk who always greeted him at the monastery. All assumptions that the monk was a kindly, gentle soul had now evaporated. They were warrior monks. As far as Jake could tell, they weren't using superpowers, but moved with supreme skill and graceful fluidity that enabled them to fight as equals. The monk's hands moved fast across Jake. He could feel stabs of pain as the monk hit several pressure points. Jake was confused about why he was suddenly being attacked. With the final prod at the back of his neck, Jake was suddenly able to move. He flexed his arms in amazement. The monks obviously knew secrets that could overcome superpowers. Could it be possible that there were even greater types of power that he wasn't aware of?

A blast of heat caught his attention. The battle had progressed further. Pete had now alighted on top of Jupiter as it orbited the orrery. The largest planet in the solar system gave him a solid platform from which he hurled dozens of blue energy spheres that dogged the monks' feet—ripping the floor up with their intensity.

Across the chamber, Lorna was using an energy shield to defend herself against multiple attacks. Jake ignored her—she was a problem to deal with another day. This was the second time she had shifted alliances, and he vowed it would be the last.

Even with no powers, Jake wasn't prepared to let Pete steal the pendants; he'd bite his ankles off if he had to. The small orb representing the downgraded ex-planet of Pluto slowly revolved towards Jake. He used the supporting gantry arm to climb onto the outer rim of the orrery. Pete was slightly higher and further towards the centre of the machine . . . and he hadn't seen Jake.

Jake used Pluto's slow orbit to position himself for a

Restoration

jump across the solar system—across Neptune's path—
landing on Uranus. His sweaty hands couldn't gain a
firm hold and he started sliding down the sphere,
which was the size of a sofa. He glanced down, suddenly conscious that the base of the orrery was a sea of
swirling gear shafts and cogs. Falling now would be like
falling into a blender . . . and he didn't have any powers
to heal himself.

His feet cycled out—his trainer finding a toehold on
the thin metal ring that surrounded the planet. It was
enough to stop him falling.

Pete suddenly swung past, balanced atop Jupiter and
on a quicker orbit than him. Pete did a double take as
Jake roared past—then shot at him.

Luck was on Jake's side. Uranus's rotation placed the
bulk of the bronze planet in between Jake and Pete.
Pete's energy spheres reverberated from the large
sphere, rocking it on its mounting. The metal ratchet
holding it together wasn't designed for such punishment. Jake leapt across the model—and landed on top
of Saturn as it swung past him. This planet was much
bigger, about the size of a truck, giving Jake a firmer
footing. Because each planet was rotating on its axis as
well as orbiting the sun, Pete had become disorientated
and lost sight of him.

'Let's go!' Pete shouted to Lorna. 'The Enforcers are
starting the air strike!'

Lorna sonic screamed at the monks attacking her, sending them reeling into the wall. She turned to give him the thumbs-up—but then noticed Jake riding the huge bronze sphere that was tracking on an intercept course for Pete.

'Watch out!' she yelled.

Pete only saw Jake when he was in mid-leap. It was a risky manoeuvre, but Jake had no other option. His aim was perfect.

He crashed into Pete who fell backwards, trying to cling on to the largest planet in the universe as he slid down the other side. Jake went straight for his hand—not to help him, but to pull the pendants free. Pete's other hand shot out, grabbing Jake's wrist. Jake's muscles twanged in agony as he suspended Pete's weight.

'Give me the pendants!'

'No way, Hunter. You're a wanted felon now. Everybody is looking for them. The word's out. Every hero, villain, and Forger is after your head! Now I've got them.'

'You want them to hunt you down too?'

'I'm not so stupid to try and use a Core Power. I'm working with people who want to stop what you've started.'

'That's exactly what I'm trying to do!'

Pete laughed. 'Oh, you're trying to play hero now? For some reason . . . I don't believe that.'

Restoration

'Give me the pendants back and once I get the others and put things right, I'll reverse the virus in you. I promise.'

Pete was surprised at the sincerity in Jake's voice, although he didn't believe a word of it.

The girder supporting Jupiter groaned under their combined weight. They both glanced at the whirling gears below in alarm. Jake tried to shake Pete free.

'Get off!'

With a reverberating CLANG, the girder suddenly snapped and the massive bronze ball dropped from its pedestal, smashing the gears beneath. A hideous sound of twisting metal filled the hall as the orrery shuddered to a halt. Jupiter began rolling towards the outer rim.

Jake was forced to walk backwards to keep his balance as the ball rolled beneath him. He only managed a couple of steps before Pete was carried under his feet like chewing gum on a football—knocking Jake over.

Jupiter smashed through the other planets, its sheer weight demolishing the intricate mechanisms. A couple of monks who were nursing wounds on the floor suddenly found a new lease of life as they scrambled to avoid being crushed.

Jake and Pete were tossed from the planet as it rolled across the floor, marble cracking under its weight. The

10110100000011001010011010101001001010

planet picked up momentum—bursting through the wall like a wrecking ball, and into another hall beyond.

Jake felt a bolt of pain shoot through his arm—he had broken it in the fall, and without a healing power he was bitterly reminded what it was like to be normal. He cradled his injury and looked around for Pete, hoping for inspiration to stop him . . . but Pete and Lorna had vanished.

As the rest of the orrery shook and rattled behind him, Jake could only stare blankly at the spot where Pete had been. He had been double-crossed by Lorna, and the pendants had been taken from him by the kid he used to bully at school.

Jake could no longer stop the moon's collision course.

He had just run out of luck.

And that's when the Enforcer air strike launched a reign of hell down on the monastery.

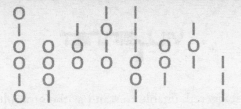

Unexpected Help

The air strike was a blur of light and noise.

The first missile struck through the roof of the main hall, destroying the curtain-draped room and creating a massive crater in the floor. The shockwave made the dividing wall crumble and hunks of masonry rained down on Jake.

The concussion blast made Jake's ears ring and he lost his balance. Another GM-65 Maverick missile tore through the ceiling of the orrery—but miraculously didn't detonate until it had passed through the opposite wall and into the courtyard beyond. The ground juddered. Planets on the mangled orrery shook from the impact—tearing from their mounts and rolling towards Jake.

Jake looked wildly around for Leech. Had he abandoned him?

He tried to weave between the large bronze balls, but his coordination was off. He dodged Uranus as it rolled past, and bounced off Mars, further injuring his broken arm.

Jake staggered, unable to stand as the ground shook. Fires broke out across the monastery, and he could feel the wall of heat from the room beyond. Chunks of roof had been torn off, admitting flurries of snow from outside—which melted in the strong black smoke updraughts coming from the building.

Powerless, Jake was convinced his number was up.

Then he felt something shoved into his hand. It was his mobile phone. He glimpsed Leech—the old man was furious as his home collapsed around him. Jake gripped the phone—just as Saturn broke free from the orrery and rolled over Leech!

Jake looked away, but he heard the crunch of bones over the scream of a jet fighter zooming low overhead. Jake didn't want to look at the damage Saturn caused, but there was no way Leech could have survived that.

Jake dropped to his knees and tried to concentrate on the phone's screen. His vision had blurred and another close explosion spewed debris over him, pushing him over.

His numb fingers just couldn't press the buttons.

Jake slumped flat on the ground, defeated.

Another explosion lifted him through the air like a crash-test dummy. He rebounded off something solid.

Darkness consumed him.

* * *

Unexpected Help

'Pete? Pete? Hello? I'm talking to you.'

Pete tore his gaze away from the pendants and finally looked at Orsina. There was a dreamy expression across his face.

'Are you OK?' she asked.

'Mmm? Yeah . . . sure. It's just, well, do you know the power I've got in my hands?'

'Of course I do. Do you realize the risks we took to get them?'

This sobered Pete up. 'Of course I do. Where's Chameleon?'

'He's on his way up. He was taunting the prisoner in the basement.' Orsina looked nervous. She was far from happy about how their plan was unfolding. 'Surely you don't trust him?' Pete gently stroked a pendant, as if expecting a genie to pop out of it. His short attention span was irritating her. 'Pete!'

'What? Oh . . . him. Why wouldn't I trust him?'

'Because of what he has done to his old friends. He abandoned you, he's turned his back on the Hero Foundation—'

'They're ancient history anyway. He can see Forge is the new power.'

'And because of what he just did to Lorna! Plus you can see the madness in his eyes. I saw him downloading from Hero.com.'

'So?'

'He's a Prime. He's not supposed to mix his powers. It's driving him crazy. He's out of control!' she hissed.

Pete looked at her suspiciously. 'Don't you think I can keep him in check?'

Orsina didn't dare speak her mind. She had heard the stories of Pete losing his temper with some other Forge members and it hadn't worked out well. 'What would Emily think?'

Pete froze. He had talked to his old friend Emily on several occasions. She had contacted him, thinking she could bring him back to the Hero Foundation to cure his illness. Emily was also Lorna's best friend, and Pete had gone out of his way to ensure the two friends didn't run into one another at Forge. Orsina could tell Pete liked her a lot.

'How would she find out?' His tone was flat, but there was no mistaking the veiled threat.

Orsina sighed with frustration. 'Can't you see how this Core Power quest is making you obsessive. You're getting hooked on its potential power. Even Jake didn't—'

Pete slammed his fist on the table. 'It's not affect-ing me,' he bellowed. 'And for your information this power . . . this could be the cure to the virus inside me!'

'That's what Chameleon told you. But how? It is gravity . . . how can that cure you?'

Pete sneered. 'You really are stupid. Core Powers

Unexpected Help

form the base of all other powers. This could be manipulated, used to create a cure!'

'It's used in flying, levitation and probably a hundred other defence and attack powers, but I can't see how it's used in healing. I think Chameleon's lying to you!'

Ever since they had heard of Jake's search for the Core Power, Forge had been researching the subject. They discovered Core Powers intoxicated those around them. The lure of such mighty power was too much for some to bear and they went crazy trying to use them.

Pete had been surprised that Jake wasn't affected, and if he was honest with himself he could feel a hazy cloud blot his reasoning skills, whispering to him about the amazing things he could achieve with such power. From what he had discovered when he hacked into the Foundation database, Leech was too weak to endure such an attachment to the powers again, and Jake had been his perfect tool to send out to retrieve them. Pete was convinced that, with experimentation, any Core Power might produce a cure to the virus Jake had unleashed in him.

Now it was a race against time. The virus was making him weaker by the day. Without a cure he would be dead. His own survival had to outweigh friendships. Even that of Emily and Lorna.

The door opened, cutting off Orsina's sharp retort.

Lorna entered with a smug smile plastered across her face.

'The Enforcers are reporting total destruction of the monastery. Nobody survived. They're sending ground troops in to make sure.'

Orsina didn't want to hear any more, and quickly left the room.

'Where are the pendants?' asked Lorna greedily.

Pete hesitated to show them. He gestured to Lorna, from head-to-toe. 'Erm . . . you staying like that?'

'Huh? Oh . . . in all the excitement, I forgot.'

With a crunch of bones and wet flesh, Lorna morphed back into Chameleon's normal form. He stretched his neck left and right, his spine clicking into place.

'That's better,' sighed Chameleon. 'Now, the pendants, if you please.'

A vague warmness roused Jake back to consciousness. He opened his mouth to speak, but could only whimper.

'Ssssh,' whispered a voice.

The darkness clouding Jake's vision slowly changed to white. It took him a moment to realize that he was staring straight up as a blizzard descended. He propped himself up on his elbows, whimpered from the pain in

Unexpected Help

his fractured arm, and slumped back against the snow. He could see the monastery about half a mile away. Most of the structure was ablaze, the strong winds fanning the flames.

A buzzing sound permeated the wind. He could see figures on snowmobiles driving up the slope towards the ruins. Jake could just make out the weapons and familiar Enforcer uniforms.

He looked up at his saviour—and was surprised to see Orsina watching the Enforcers from their vantage point on a plateau. Her hands were glowing bright red, melting the snow around him, and providing the warmth so neither froze to death.

'What . . . ?' Jake managed.

'We don't have much time. Can you use your phone and download powers? You need to get fighting fit and you need to do it fast.'

Jake's trembling good hand wiped the frost off the phone's screen. He was relieved to see the phone was still working despite the temperature. He selected a strong healing factor and immediately felt waves of warmth course through his body, repairing internal bleeding, cracked bones, and torn muscles. His whole body made peculiar crunching noises as everything reset itself.

He clambered to his knees and watched the Enforcers who were now combing through the rubble.

'Leech . . .'

Orsina laid a restraining hand on his shoulder. 'Take it easy. I haven't seen Leech anywhere. I'm not sure if he got out.'

Jake hung his head. 'I saw him crushed to death next to me.'

'I didn't see the body, but there was not much left of the building for him to have hidden in. And in a couple of minutes, the Enforcers will be announcing that you are dead too. They knew you didn't have any powers and since everybody in the world is hunting the Dark Hunter, who would be stupid enough to attempt a rescue?'

Jake looked sidelong at her, but she was staring at the ruins. 'Why did you rescue me?'

Pete's glazed expression had frightened her, and Chameleon's duplicity had convinced her that she was on the wrong side of things. Orsina had once been a member of the Foundation, but had left when she started to disagree with the direction the organization was taking. She had hoped Forge would provide the world with the protection it needed. Her new home had been great, until Jake had triggered the virus in Pete and Chameleon had turned up. Now she was convinced Forge was no better than the Council of Evil, run by two dictators. Bizarrely, she saw Jake now as the only hope to stop all three super-players from letting the world fall apart as they squabbled amongst themselves.

'Because . . . because what they did to you wasn't right. I joined Forge to get away from all that political double-crossing, and that's exactly what Chameleon is turning it into.'

'Chameleon? But he's Foundation . . .'

'He's left. He didn't agree with Kirby's methods. Now he's using Pete's stupidity to help him steal the pendants from you. Sure, he'll probably stop the path of destruction you started . . . but then he'll use the pendants for his own wants and desires. You were different. The Core Powers never affected you in the same way. They usually turn people crazy with power lust. I can see them starting to affect Pete. Only the stronger willed can resist, like Necros and Kirby. And, surprisingly, you.'

Jake didn't pick up on the subtle insult. He had suddenly remembered Lorna's betrayal. Next time he saw her . . . she would pay.

'Is Lorna with them?'

Orsina hesitated. She wanted to tell Jake the truth. Tell him that Chameleon had taken Lorna prisoner, and placed her in the Forge dungeons. Then he impersonated Lorna when he arrived at Jake's house. She should tell him . . . but Lorna had been a bit of a jealous pain, and Orsina was starting to like Jake, and it meant her competition was safely behind bars. She changed the subject.

'We need to leave.'

'Where are we going?'

'To Forge. Pete's computer worked out the correct sequence to align the powers so they can control them properly. In a couple of minutes they will assemble the pendants to vanquish the black hole. After that, we must get them back.'

'They can't.'

'Can't what?'

'They can't get rid of the black hole even if they correctly assemble the wand. Do you really think I *wanted* to hurl the moon into the earth? I'm not crazy! The only way of truly mastering the power is with all six parts. All they will do is probably open another one . . .'

He trailed off as they both realized the deadly implications.

'It doesn't fit properly. This one's got a slight ridge.'

'Let me try,' said Pete, gently nudging Chameleon out of the way. He looked at the instructions on the monitor and pushed the two parts of the pendant together, but they repelled each other like similar magnetic poles on a magnet. He caught the pendant before it sprang across the room.

Unexpected Help

'Wait, I see. These two symbols are slightly different,' Chameleon pointed out on the screen. He eased the pendants from Pete and tried another combination with the same result. 'If Hunter can do it, it must be fairly basic stuff.'

The door opened and a young Forge member stepped in—abruptly stopping when he saw the thunderous expression on Chameleon's and Pete's faces.

'What?' snapped Pete. 'Can't you see we're busy?'

'Um . . . Chameleon wanted to know the moment we heard reports about the Dark Hunter . . .'

'Chameleon doesn't give the orders around here. I do!' bellowed Pete.

'It's OK, Pete.' Chameleon's voice was calm, which added to undermining Pete's aggressive attitude. An attitude he had fostered after watching TV shows about successful business people. Apparently they were all unpleasant. 'What have you heard?'

The kid smiled, relieved not to be shouted at. 'Dark Hunter is dead. It's all across the networks we've intercepted.'

Pete smirked. He felt zero remorse for the boy who had made his life a living hell while at school. Chameleon felt odd. He had dreamt about getting his revenge on Hunter, but hearing the news and not actually being the one who caused it felt disappointing. He had lost an enemy who, despite his ambivalent feelings of hatred and loathing towards him, had been his equal.

The kid hurried out of the room, leaving them to absorb the news.

'Hurry up,' said Pete.

Chameleon pulled himself together. He didn't want to show any weakness in front of Pete. Chameleon glanced at the diagram on screen and suddenly realized what they were doing wrong. He flipped the end of one of the pendants he was holding and it suddenly snapped together. Both parts began to glow.

'It's working! That means the other two should be straightforward.'

Chameleon clung onto the glowing sections as Pete delicately applied the third pendant. He felt it pluck from his fingers as he got close, and lock into place.

'This is it,' breathed Chameleon. Greed glinted in his eyes. 'Now, the last piece. Hurry!'

Pete hesitated. 'Why don't I hold it and you lock the last piece in?'

'Does it matter?'

'If it doesn't matter then let's swap.'

Chameleon narrowed his eyes and tried to pull the last piece from Pete's hand. 'We haven't got time to mess around! Give it to me!'

Pete quickly pulled away.

Chameleon sighed. 'Look, it doesn't matter who is

Unexpected Help

holding the thing. The power radiates out and we're both here. Just do it.'

Pete had never entirely trusted Chameleon from the first moment they had met, but they were all running out of time and he was relying on Chameleon to keep his word and help cure him. Reluctantly, Pete attached the end segment. It clicked into place, and the whole array suddenly glowed brightly.

'We've got it!' said Chameleon in awe.

He started to rise up from the ground, giggling as he did so. 'See? Flying . . . that uses part of this power. It's incredible, I—'

A radioactive green sphere hit Chameleon so hard he dropped the wand as he was smashed through three sets of reinforced steel walls, falling outside the Forge HQ. The wand rolled towards the door.

Jake and Orsina quantum tunnelled into the room and Jake shot another radioactive bolt at Pete. The impact hit Pete square in the chest, knocking him into the corner of the room. The blows didn't damage him. Pete had the uncanny ability to absorb the energy. His body reacted by growing in bulk. His clothes stretched as he did—Pete had long ago worked out that he had to wear expanding clothes since he was tired of being naked in the middle of a superpowered showdown.

Orsina headed for the computer to download the pendant data.

Jake ran for the assembled pendants.

Pete held up his hand—and the pendant wand telekinetically leapt into his palm.

'Mine,' he growled.

'Trust me, Prof,' said Jake, using the detested nickname he had given Pete, 'you have no idea what you're doing.'

Pete flicked the power-pendant in Jake's direction. A swirling cone extended out for two metres, creating a powerful suction that hurled everything towards it.

Jake was plucked off his feet, but his hand snagged the doorjamb, supporting him. Orsina swept through the air, grabbing Jake's leg at the very last moment.

A table, chair, and computer were the first items sucked into the vortex. The further they drifted down the cone, the smaller they got—compressed by gravity into nothing bigger than ball bearings before they vanished.

Jake could feel his belt was beginning to unbuckle from Orsina's weight—she would fall into the vortex with his jeans if he didn't do something.

The wood around the door cracked as it started to give in to the relentless assault. Jake knew if he shook Orsina free it would buy him more time, but he couldn't bring himself to abandon the person who had just saved him from certain death.

Wall, ceiling, and floor panels worked loose and were

swept into oblivion. One smashed in half across Jake's head—almost making him lose his grip.

Holding on to the splintering frame, he tried to fly forwards, but his power wasn't strong enough to counteract the vortex.

He squinted above Pete—dual beams shooting from his eyes, cutting a circle in the roof above Pete. An entire section of the floor above—complete with a couch, TV, and console, which was being played by two Forge members—fell onto Pete, crushing him to the floor and extinguishing the wand's power.

The two Forge members stared at Jake in astonishment—before one fired lightning bolts from his fingers.

Orsina moved so fast she appeared at the attacker's side and knocked him out with a punch. The remaining Forge member turned and fled, flying through the hole left by Chameleon.

Orsina reached for the wand—but was knocked off her feet as Pete flung the wreckage of the sofa and TV at her. She moved quickly enough to avoid being splattered—but that positioned her at the end of the room.

The attack had made Pete swell even bigger.

'Like a cockroach, you just won't die, will you?' he bellowed at Jake.

'Is that any way to talk about your old friend?'

Jake and Pete moved for the pendant-wand at the

same time—and grabbed either end. They invoked the power simultaneously—

A gravitational force welled up—blasting a huge section of roof away above them as an invisible wave shot out so fast that the clouds mustering above were dispersed like smoke.

They wrestled for the pendants. Despite Pete's greater bulk, their strength was equally matched. The gravity rod swung one way—then another. A monumental gravity force washed out—taking out one entire wall of Forge's headquarters, which included a high-powered server room. Both wall and servers were hurled a hundred miles across the Rocky Mountains and into the farmlands of Montana, where they smashed through a barn and startled many chickens.

The wave swept in the other direction, ripping the building's generator off its concrete foundations with ease. The gravitation force was so immense that the generator soared clean into Canada, landing in a lake.

Still, neither gained control of the pendants.

A massive hand suddenly gripped around Pete's chest—fingers the width of thick rope. He was hoisted in the air, the pendant slipping from Jake's grasp. Now Jake could see Chameleon was hovering just outside the remains of the base. His arm extended, growing disproportionately in size so he could hold Pete up with little effort.

Unexpected Help

'That's mine!' he snarled.

'You traitor!' shouted Pete. 'Here—have this instead!'

He flicked the rod at Chameleon. A small black ball shot out and hovered between them for a moment before it exploded into a tiny black hole, no bigger than a cup.

Every item of debris in the area was sucked towards it. Jake's feet skidded on the floor as he struggled, yet again, against being pulled into the hole. Only Pete and Chameleon were unaffected. Pete looked at the shape-changer quizzically.

'Anti-gravity,' smiled Chameleon ruefully. 'Apparently your new toy is useless against me.'

Jake managed to distance himself from the immediate pull of the mini black hole, although the air roared around his ears. He watched Chameleon and Pete lunge for one another—Chameleon using his new downloaded powers to swat Pete aside.

'Like it? Got it from Villain.net,' snarled Chameleon. 'Some cool stuff on there.' That confirmed he was mixing his natural powers with downloaded ones, something no Prime had ever successfully done before.

Jake could have kicked himself for not planning ahead. He had seen the anti-grav power on the V-Net system. Back at the Council he had once scrolled through every icon, asking technicians what they meant. He tried to recall the icon for anti-gravity as the two Supers battled behind him. The black hole vanished with a loud pop, and now they were hurling fireballs at one another.

Across the rubble, Jake could see Orsina hiding. She glanced at him—and he suddenly heard her voice as she telepathically talked to him.

'What do we do?' It was as loud and clear as if she was standing next to him. Jake didn't know how to respond, he didn't have telepathy and he didn't want to shout the plan across the room. Sometimes girls just didn't think things through, they . . .

'I can hear your thoughts, you know, doofus.'

Jake blushed and tried to clear his mind. He glanced at the struggling Supers. Pete had Chameleon pinned down but they both had their hands on the wand, which was glowing so brightly that neither could look at it. Gravity waves snaked out, resembling electric blue streamers that made everything they struck rise to the ceiling.

A plan formed in Jake's mind, which, telepathically, Orsina suddenly understood. Jake liked the way she was easy to talk to—but immediately regretted thinking that she was really cool . . . and quite cute. Luckily she didn't reply, and Jake hoped she had been out of his head.

Orsina spurred forwards at lightning speed. All she had to do was knock the pendant from their hands so

Unexpected Help

Jake could swoop in and pick it up. She didn't want to touch it herself, just in case the power started to corrupt her own morals.

She was fast—but didn't know about one of Einstein's revelations. Gravity had a peculiar effect on time.

From her point of view, travelling fast simply meant that the rest of the world appeared to slow to a crawl. To Orsina, it could take minutes to cover a mile, but everybody else would see her cover the distance in seconds.

She bore in on her target. As a keen football player she was ready to boot the wand from their greedy hands. However, as fast as the rest of the world seemed, the gravity waves still moved as fast as they had done in real-time. There was no way to avoid them. Just as she was centimetres away, a streamer struck out—hitting her in the face.

Jake saw Orsina vanish—almost instantly appearing next to the duelling ex-heroes as a streamer hit her. It didn't cause any physical damage, but instantly made her lighter than gravity. She began to rapidly rise in the air—her arms and legs windmilling in a futile attempt to stop her ascent.

'Aargh! Help me!'

Jake hesitated. Pete appeared to be winning the battle on the ground and Orsina seemed to be accelerating the further she rose. If she didn't stop then she would be ejected from the planet and hurled into space.

'Why does stuff like this always happen to me?' grumbled Jake before he shot in the air in pursuit.

Orsina was facing the ground as she rose and saw Jake hurtle towards her . . . but he appeared to slow down.

'What're you doing? Help me!'

From Jake's point of view Orsina was rising ever faster and he couldn't keep up. A quick glance down revealed they had already cleared the top of the highest mountain peak in the vicinity. The air was becoming very cold.

Jake was flying as fast as he could. Perhaps if he had the ability to create new powers, he could have pushed himself faster, but on downloaded energy he was running flat-out.

His hands and face started to sting as his skin frosted over. Orsina was far ahead and accelerating. Jake assumed she would freeze to death before she punctured through the atmosphere.

There was only one thing he could do.

He stopped dead in the air.

Orsina peeled upwards, faster than her screams could reach Jake. Jake formed an energy bubble around himself; took a deep breath; and hurtled back towards the ground.

Unexpected Help

Pete was throttling Chameleon. The shapeshifter was rapidly morphing under his grip, but Pete wasn't letting go. The pendant finally slipped from Chameleon's grasp. Pete rolled aside and picked it up, ready to strike Chameleon.

'A-ha!' he exclaimed victoriously.

Just as a whooshing noise caught Pete's attention. He glanced up to see Jake descending so quickly that the friction around his energy bubble turned into intense flames.

Jake was on course to slam into Chameleon at close to the speed of sound. The floor ripped away in a massive crater, Forge headquarters quivering from the violent impact. Pete couldn't fly in his enlarged state, so was forced to leap aside as a shock wave rolled across the floor, toppling more internal walls.

Then silence.

Pete cautiously edged to the hole in the floor as steam rose. Jake had splintered through some of the stilts holding the building onto the side of the mountain, and even through the bedrock below. Pete could see a smouldering crater, but there was no sign of Chameleon or Jake. Pete wondered it they had been incinerated on impact.

Then he felt a shock to his back and suddenly found he was paralysed.

Jake walked into Pete's field of view and snatched

the pendant from his hand. He concentrated and held it aloft—sending a gravity streamer upwards, hoping it would strike Orsina. Then he turned to Pete.

'You have no idea what I'm about to do to you.'

Pete felt pangs of fear. The very same ones he had experienced when Jake had bullied him at school and given him a wedgie. They now felt like certain death.

'The worst thing was . . . whatever you did to make Lorna betray me.'

Pete wanted to plead that Lorna was safe and had no idea about the deceitful act Chameleon had conjured up . . . it was possibly the only thing that could save his life, but he couldn't move his tongue.

Jake was iridescent with rage. 'You know what I'm going to do to you to make you pay? Nothing. Nothing at all.'

Pete liked the sound of that, but couldn't express his relief.

Jake continued. 'That virus I put inside you . . . that's going to eat you from the inside. Painfully. And you'll be permanently paralysed so there is nothing you can do about it except just stand there and endure it. Watching your extremities get eaten away and feeling every moment of pain.'

Jake had no idea if that was true or not. He knew the virus would kill him eventually, but it would probably be a painless poisoning. He knew he should feel bad for

Unexpected Help

the pain he was causing, but his old bully instincts were still alive and well. Besides, how could he forgive somebody who had tried to kill his parents?

However, he planned to keep Pete permanently encased in an amber block, as he had done to Chameleon once before. At least he would suffer under the belief it would be painful. Psychological torture was just an effective bullying device.

Jake suddenly heard whistling. He looked up to see Orsina in free fall. He remembered that she had no flying powers. He extended the pendant-wand and she abruptly stopped a metre above the floor, unconscious.

Jake ran to her side and gently lowered her to the ground. Her face was covered in frost, her lips tinged blue. He felt for a pulse, and picked up the faintest trace.

With trembling hands, Jake held his phone close to her face and accessed a healing power. The light strobed across her skin . . . but nothing happened.

Jake panicked. She couldn't die . . . he wouldn't let her. He gripped the Core Powers . . . but they could do nothing to fight life and death. That was another power altogether.

'Orsina, don't die. Please.' It was a lame thing to say, but it made him feel less helpless. Then he recalled that the Villain.net system used to transfer the superpowers through a finger of energy that flexed out of the screen; the new system relied on looking at the screen as the powers were strobed into the Downloader's eye.

He forced one of Orsina's eyelids open with one hand and accessed V-net with the other. The power strobed into her eyes, and he immediately saw her pupils dilate.

Her breathing slowly became stronger and colour came back to her face. Jake couldn't help but smile as her eyes opened.

'Did we get it?' she asked weakly.

Jake held up the pendants. 'Got it.' He turned to gloat some more at Pete—but he was missing.

Jake leapt to his feet, searching the area, expecting Pete to leap out at any moment in an ambush. But there was no sign of him.

Puzzled, Jake knelt next to Orsina.

'Where are they?'

'Pete vanished, and I suspect Chameleon teleported away just before I could pound him. We should leave. I've got a bad feeling about this.'

He helped her stand.

'It won't take long for the Council or Foundation to detect that gravity pulse either,' she warned. 'Then they will be here like a shot to take the pendants. And I don't think I can fight much more. Where's my phone?' she added urgently.

Unexpected Help

They found it amongst the debris. Orsina smiled as she checked it was working.

'Good news,' she said, holding the screen for Jake to see. The pendant's correct assembly instructions spun slowly round. 'I bluetoothed it off the system.'

'Excellent.' That wouldn't have occurred to Jake. However, his good mood didn't last for long and his smile vanished. 'But the worst is yet to come. Kirby has one pendant and Necros has the other. Without them we can't stop the moon from colliding with the earth.'

They instinctively looked up. Even in the daylight, the moon was clearly visible, much larger than it should be.

Jake's phone suddenly vibrated. He glanced at the damaged screen. Somebody had sent him a video message. Perhaps Lorna, begging for forgiveness?

He accessed it—and almost dropped the phone when Eric Kirby's face appeared on the screen.

'Hello, Jake. I believe I have something you are looking for?' Kirby held up the pendant that was around his neck. 'We should meet to talk. As surprising as this sounds . . . *I need your help.*'

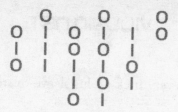

Cairo

Chameleon glanced at the prone figure on the floor next to him. He was experiencing a sudden rush of guilt, which he held in check when he reminded himself of what was at stake.

'This is the right thing to do,' he whispered to himself.

Perhaps he had used a little too much force on the prone hero lying on the floor, but he couldn't run the risk of being discovered. He hadn't officially left the Foundation, but it was clear in his mind that the organization was inward facing and not going anywhere. Eric Kirby had built up a formidable power that could have long since vanquished the villains of this world, but he had refused to do so as if some higher authority was holding him back.

Chameleon had had enough. He had to take matters into his own hands for the good of the planet. He was still alive, stronger than ever and convinced that it was because he was mixing powers from Hero.com and Villain.net, something he knew no Prime should try.

He needed every trick up his sleeve to stop the Dark Hunter.

The Gravity Core Power was not safe in Hunter's hand, and Chameleon was baffled as to why neither the Foundation nor Council had sent any major task-force to retrieve it. Chameleon had played by the rules when he had used the Enforcers to take Hunter out— but as usual, they had failed.

Chameleon's path was clear. Claim the Core Power, reverse the moon's destructive path, and then make Forge the single superpower that would strike at the heart of evil in a way the Foundation never did. Chameleon didn't see it as a political coup; he saw it as his duty.

He had sneaked back into the Foundation, although he knew there was no real need for his furtive actions, as nobody knew his plan. He'd heard loud music coming from the control room. It sounded as if a party was taking place. Chameleon felt instantly angry: what did the fools possibly have to celebrate as the world fell apart around them?

He headed straight for the subterranean bunker facility deep under the main building. Amid the back-up servers and raw powers held in a bombproof hall, the Foundation kept some of its secrets and mistakes.

Chameleon counted through the wide aisles, until he came to Row 33. At the end of the passage lay a single

Cairo

door. Frost covered the metal, even on the outside. He ran his hand over the viewing window, clearing a layer of accumulated ice. A huge dark shadow could be seen beyond. Cryogenically frozen to place out of harm's way.

Chameleon's hand danced across the keypad built into the wall. As Kirby's second-in-command, he knew all the high-level access codes.

It was time to start throwing *everything* he could at Jake Hunter.

The moon hung larger than ever in the night sky, and was now often visible in the daytime too. Twice as large, features never seen before with the naked eye became clear on the pitted grey surface.

The celestial sphere had already passed the small black hole lurking just beyond Earth's orbit. Without any other influence, the moon would have started to orbit the black hole, like a soap bubble circling the drain until it was inexorably pulled into the hole's event horizon and destroyed for ever. However, the earth's own gravity had now hooked the moon and was reeling it in at speed that was increasing with every passing hour.

Across the earth, the close moon was having devastating effects on the weather. Tides had gone crazy.

One side of the planet was experiencing extreme low tides. In some instances the water had pulled back beyond the horizon, exposing delicate coral reefs. At the same time, on the other side of the planet, oceans bulged causing extraordinary high tides that flooded the coastlines like a tsunami—destroying cities, nature reserves, and farmland.

Animal behaviour was changing as the shadow of the moon was cast over the ground. Birds endlessly flocked, confused by the intense glow of the moon, while domesticated dogs howled around the clock.

While half the planet's electronic systems were out due to supervillain activity, the half that had been functioning began to short circuit as the planet's magnetic field reacted to the moon's proximity, threatening to flip the magnetic poles—a disaster that could wipe out the world's electronic systems.

Intense sunlight burnt Jake's brow. This time he had remembered his sleek designer shades, but had forgotten his cap. At least he remembered the suntan lotion. When he had possessed his mutating powers, he had been unable to stand even weak sunlight. However, now those powers had apparently gone, so had their side effects, which meant he was now able to enjoy the heat on his skin.

Cairo

He stood on top of the central Khafre pyramid in Giza, Egypt. It offered a stunning view of the desert ahead, the other two pyramids of Khufu and Menkaure either side of him, constructed slightly out of alignment from one another in an arrangement that had puzzled archaeologists for years, until it was discovered they were built in exactly the same layout as the constellation of Orion's belt.

Behind him lay the back of the impressive, and noseless, Sphinx, a silent guardian to the netherworld, beyond which was the uninspiring view of downtown Cairo, where the desert suddenly ended in a sprawling mass of tower blocks and urbanization.

Orsina stood next to him, arms windmilling to steady herself atop the steep slope of the pyramid's apex. Her NY Yankees cap protected her from the desert sun.

'I don't like this, Jake. I don't like it one little bit. It smells like a trap to me.'

They had discussed the pros and cons of believing Eric Kirby's video message. Why would the leader of a super-power want to speak to Jake, who was still his enemy?

Jake knew that the Foundation wasn't functioning properly, and they had both seen Chameleon go crazy, and heard his ravings. On that basis, Kirby's request didn't seem so strange.

On the other hand, Orsina speculated that

Chameleon's craziness could just be an elaborate ruse designed to lure Jake into a false sense of security so he could steal the pendants from him.

The flaw to this argument was the fact that Chameleon had already taken the powers, and they had both seen him grow corrupt with the thought of such immense power in his hands. That had been no act.

Before they had left the Rockies, Orsina had left Jake sifting through the debris for any further information on the pendants while she ran around the remains of the Forge building, under the pretence of looking for survivors. She had felt bad about keeping Lorna locked away, and had freed her.

Luckily, Lorna blamed Pete and Chameleon for her incarceration and was relieved to be free again. Especially as she had been helpless when the building collapsed around her.

Orsina had copied the Forge data onto Jake's phone, and handed Lorna her own. With it, Lorna was able to log on to Forge's servers, which fortunately operated from another site, so she could access Hero.com. Orsina was feeling guilty about the way she had treated Lorna and had tried to interfere with her relationship with Jake. To make amends she had vowed to help her. She quickly briefed Lorna that the phone contained the history of the pendants that Pete had downloaded from the Foundation. She had a sneaking suspicion that there was more information there that would prove useful.

Orsina had made sure Lorna teleported away before she could ask any awkward questions about Jake. Then she had joined Jake and they had prepared for Cairo.

Jake glanced above. The huge moon hung in the morning sky. When replenishing his powers on V-net, he had read news reports that the moon was already casting a permanent shadow over parts of the world, spurring superstitious people into madness. *Lunatics* was the buzzword, taken from the origin of the word.

'I can't see anyone,' commented Orsina. 'Not even tourists.'

Jake's thoughts drifted from Chameleon, to Lorna and the girl standing next to him. He cleared his throat, which felt dry in the desert air.

'Don't take this the wrong way . . . but how do I know you are not part of all this? Part of a back-up plan to try and win my confidence, just in case it all goes wrong? Lorna let me down . . . why shouldn't you?'

Again, another opportunity to tell the truth about Lorna passed by. Orsina shrugged. 'I guess you can't know that for sure.'

It wasn't the denial Jake was expecting, and although it was a vague answer, it was somehow reassuring.

Jake gave the area one last sweep. He could see no Foundation or Enforcer vehicles anywhere, unless they were hidden in the suburbs. Maybe Kirby had come alone as he had said in the video message.

'Let's go.'

For reasons he couldn't fathom, several downloaded powers refused to stick to Jake's system. He was still having problems flying, and a couple of his favourite attack powers were nothing more than damp squibs. He needed to get somebody to look at how the EMP had altered his body—the last thing he needed was his body rejecting every superpower. That would be a disaster.

Jake apported behind the Sphinx: the power was only suitable over short distances. He had to jump again to arrive in between the statue's extended front legs. Orsina joined him seconds later with her super-speed.

They gazed up at the weather-worn sculpture. Scaffolding had been erected to one side as conservation efforts tried to repair the damage from wind erosion. At one point, the desert sands reached up to the shoulders, which had helped sandblast the details on the face away.

Around them stood the remains of ancient buildings known as the Temple of the Sphinx, with the Valley Temple of Khafre adjacent to them. Once magnificent structures, they were now nothing more than ruins. A reminder of how even the most powerful empires could tumble.

A whispering voice suddenly caught Jake's attention. Orsina was about to speak, but Jake put his hand over her mouth, and a finger across his lips.

Somebody was making a phone call. Curious, Jake tiptoed towards the ruins. An opening passed into what once would have been a splendid hall. The remaining stone blocks were huge, and many interior walls stood much taller than Jake and were open to the blue skies above.

Jake crept inside, the sand smothering his footsteps. The voice grew louder as he approached a wall . . . then it suddenly fell silent mid-sentence, as if the speaker sensed Jake.

Jake's heart hammered in his chest. He knew he had to face Kirby as the fate of the world hung in the balance, but he wasn't looking forward to the encounter, even if Kirby had invited him. Jake took a deep breath and turned the corner.

'Hello, Jake,' said Eric Kirby.

Jake eyed the old man cautiously. He had seen pictures and video of the creator of Hero.com, but in the flesh, he didn't look quite as old as he had expected. Kirby leant on a cane, which Jake knew was just a prop. A lethal sword was concealed within it.

1
9
5
0
1
0
0
0
0
1
0
0
1
0
1
0
1
1
1
0
0
1
0
0
1
1
0
1

'So what now?' was all Jake could think of saying.

Orsina stood behind Jake. Kirby politely nodded.

'Ah, Ms Moretti. A pleasure.'

Orsina was surprised. 'You know me?'

'I know everybody who passes within the Foundation, even if they feel restricted by our rules and decide to leave for Forge.'

Orsina felt her cheeks burn. It was like being told off by the headmaster.

Kirby's steel gaze moved back to Jake. 'Do you have the four pendants?'

Jake thought about lying, but didn't see the point. You didn't get to be the leader of one of the most powerful organizations on Earth by being fooled by a young boy.

Jake licked his lips as his mouth was uncomfortably dry. 'You know I do. And you?'

Kirby smiled. 'Straight to the point. You really are quite a forceful chap, just like they say you are. Yes. I have mine. You are aware that all six are needed to prevent this disaster you have set in motion?'

Jake wanted to snap back that it wasn't his fault . . . but everybody knew it was. He nodded. 'And Necros has the last one.'

'Ah, yes. Necros. He's quite a foe. Powerful, very powerful. But often you will find your worst enemies are those closest to you. The ones you trust.'

Lorna popped into Jake's mind, and he trembled with anger.

Kirby stared at Jake as if he saw his future. 'The most powerful opponents are often the most easily beaten,' he said enigmatically. 'Chameleon was the Foundation's second-in-command. A firm believer in justice and doing things by the rulebook. However, it turns out that if he doesn't like the rulebook he is following then he chooses another. Or worse, writes his own. And that's such a shame. Such a waste of talent.'

'I've never really been his biggest fan,' said Jake sarcastically. To his surprise, Kirby smiled.

'I think the feeling is mutual. I've been watching your progress with interest, Jake.'

The desert heat and increasing feeling of anxiety was making Jake feel irritable. He didn't want to listen to a sermon, he just wanted to get the fight over with. 'And you've been unable to stop me.'

'Stop you? That was never my intention. I just wanted to make sure you didn't harm others.'

'You wanted to experiment on me, to find out how I was able to create new powers! You wanted to kill me!'

Kirby nodded amiably. 'Well, not kill you. But certainly get under your skin to find out what made you unique. And if the Foundation couldn't do that, then falling into the Council's fold was the best way to keep you out of harm's way. That's why I arranged it with Necros.'

Jake's chain of thought suddenly derailed. 'Arranged it? How can you arrange that?'

Kirby's gaze focused on nothing as he marshalled his thoughts. 'The Foundation and Council are two sides of the same coin. Ultimately they can each do unique things. To make sure the world doesn't fall apart, a select group called the Inner Circle watch over things. Both Necros and I are part of that.'

'You're friends?' asked Jake incredulously.

Kirby laughed. 'Hardly. In fact, Necros was quite happy to have me . . . retire from active life . . . '

It took Jake a moment to work out that was a euphemism. 'He wanted to kill you?'

'He wouldn't kill me himself, but he would be quite happy to step back and let somebody else do it. My death would bring about a much needed change to things. The Inner Circle is the reason the Core Power you have was split across the world between both sides. It was the reason I was able to give my brother's son to Necros to be raised, which, of course, you know all about. It's all boils down to politics.'

'Politics are boring,' said Jake, thinking of how his parents got so excited every time there was an election.

Kirby laughed. 'Indeed. But that's what makes the world turn. Which side are you on?'

'I'm on my side.'

Kirby treated him to a long hard look. Then eventually nodded. 'That's what makes you so different, Jake. You really are on your own side. The lure the Core Power offers doesn't affect you. That is a very rare quality.'

'I just want to stop the disaster, put things right.'

'And destroy the Foundation and Council in the process?' said Kirby with a knowing smile.

Jake nodded. 'After all the trouble they caused me? Totally.'

Kirby prodded the sand with his cane. 'That's not the solution, Jake. As I said, they are two sides of the same coin. No matter how much you chop the coin in half, it still retains two sides. Chameleon has left the Foundation; he thinks I have led it to ruin. And perhaps he is correct. However, he plans to turn Forge into the new face of heroes. As Ms Moretti will attest, that is not the point of Forge at all. The Inner Circle have forced me out of the Foundation . . .' Jake was about to interrupt, but Kirby headed off his question. 'The Inner Circle are more powerful than you can imagine. Necros and I are the weak links in that organization. I don't trust Necros as far as I could throw him. I know, like me, he couldn't resist the lure of the pendants. Which, bizarrely, leaves the Dark Hunter to save the day. That is why I am going to give you my pendant.'

Jake was instantly suspicious. 'You'll give it to me?'

Kirby held up his cane and indicated the end. The pendant was suspended in a glass orb on the tip.

'And you don't even have to kill me for it,' said Kirby with a knowing smile. 'You see, I know how my own brother thinks. He wanted me dead.'

Jake nodded in agreement. 'And now he's dead. Killed when the Enforcers attacked.'

He studied Kirby's face for a reaction. There was none.

'You are aware that there are six Core Powers in all?' said Kirby suddenly.

'Yes. Gravity, the time manipulation Lord Eon had ... what are the others?'

Kirby smiled. 'They are too powerful for you to consider right now. Core Powers can do the impossible, Jake. Remember that.'

Jake felt as if he was taking part in two different conversations. He pulled it back on track.

'So if you give me your pendant, what's the catch?'

'The catch? The only catch is that you still have to get the piece from Necros, and he won't willingly give it. You have to promise me you will avert this disaster, Jake. It's ironic; the most wanted villain in the world is now the planet's only hope for salvation.'

That made Jake smile. He was still on guard, but something told him that Kirby was telling him the truth. If he had walked into a trap then it would have been sprung immediately.

Kirby closed his eyes and clutched his temples. 'They're coming,' he said urgently.

Jake remembered that Leech and Kirby shared the power that allowed them to view events around the world.

'Who is?'

'*Everybody.*'

It was a terrifying scene. From the south, dust plumes rose as a platoon of Enforcer tanks crested sand dunes. They had taken the long way round in an attempt not to be seen. Gunship helicopters flew low over the armoured column.

From the north and east, and the sprawl of Cairo, figures came in 4x4s, motorbikes, flying, or on foot using super-speed, racing towards the pyramids.

They were Forge neutrals, heroes and villains—Primes and Downloaders—using whatever they could to reach the scene first. They were all prepared to fight to the death for the ultimate prize.

The more experienced Supers suddenly appeared around the Giza site in a cacophony of thunderclaps as they teleported in. Others quantum tunnelled. One set of foes appeared opposite each other and raced out of their portals, only to run into the open tunnel opposite. Before they realized their mistake, a group of villains had found themselves in the Foundation headquarters while a budding group of amateur heroes walked straight into the Council of Evil's assembly chamber.

Jake, Orsina, and Kirby stood on the highest wall they could find to see the madness heading towards them.

'This is nuts!' said Jake. For the first time in his life, he was experiencing stark terror.

'Every one of them wants the pendants. They want to save the world . . . then they want to use the power for themselves, which will ultimately destroy it.' Kirby gave Jake a meaningful glance. 'They must not have it, Jake. It's up to you. You're the only one who can put things right.'

'I'm not a hero,' snapped Jake.

'You are today. Sometimes, even bad guys can be heroes, Jake.'

'We can't fight them all!' said Orsina. Her voice trembled with panic. 'I didn't sign up for this . . . I shouldn't be here.'

'I can teleport away,' said Jake confidently.

'Not any more,' said Kirby. 'You see those Enforcer vehicles?' He pointed to a line of fast-moving trucks that raced over the dunes on caterpillar tracks. A sphere was mounted on the roof of each. 'Dampener trucks. The latest Enforcer weapon. There are too many assault powers for them to be able to dampen them all, so they concentrate on specific powers: tele-portation, apporting and tunnelling. That way they can effectively trap their enemy. We won't be able to leave the area—we got here just before they acti-vated the machines. We're all trapped. They're very effective. I helped design them,' he added with a trace of pride.

'Great. You've helped get us killed.'

A voice suddenly echoed across the ruins, closer than the approaching mob. 'Hunter!!'

'There!' exclaimed Orsina, pointing to the Sphinx.

Chameleon stood on the Sphinx's head, staring down at Jake.

'There you are! And Kirby? You too? This is unex-pected.'

'I came to put a stop to your madness,' said Kirby levelly. He was calm, not betraying the slightest worry that they were surrounded by hordes of angry Supers. 'You still have time to give yourself up and come back to the Foundation for some conditioning therapy.'

'You mean mind control?' scoffed Chameleon. 'Just like he did to Jake's sister,' he addressed Jake directly. 'Speaking of whom . . . '

Beth suddenly landed with a thump on one of the

Sphinx's paws. She looked a little puzzled at seeing Kirby standing with the enemy.

'Commander Courage?' she used Kirby's superhero name. 'What . . . ?'

Chameleon interrupted her. 'I told you, Kirby is a traitor.'

Beth looked crestfallen.

Kirby shook his head in wonder. 'You have become a liar, too? How did this happen?'

'You have destroyed the Foundation! I'm going to put things right now!'

Two figures suddenly landed on the ruins of the Khafre temple, close to Jake. Jake was alarmed to see it was Pete and his old hero friend, Emily.

Pete glanced around in astonishment. The Enforcer tanks were spreading out just beyond the pyramids. Their choppers circled noisily around, attacking the horde of approaching Supers. An assortment of energy projectiles: lightning, fireballs, and streams of plasma shot out in all directions as the battle started. The Enforcers retaliated with rockets that blasted the approaching vehicles.

'Wow,' said Pete. 'This is going to be one heck of a party.'

With a bass-heavy thrum, the ground started to shake. Several metres away, a patch of sand suddenly turned black as it fused into glass. Then it shattered and a hulking figure leapt out with smoke rising from his black ceramic plated suit.

'Hunter! You've betrayed the Council. I have evidence that you assassinated Amy, Mobius, and Armageddon! Your treachery has been uncovered and you will pay!'

An all-encasing helmet concealed the newcomer's face, but the four lupine eye slits, two pairs just above one another, could only belong to one of the surviving Council of Evil members:

'Fallout!' growled Jake.

Fallout was about to make a witty remark when he suddenly became aware of the stand-off developing around him.

'What the hell is going on?' he demanded.

'It seems Jake has just about managed to annoy the entire planet,' quipped Chameleon.

Fallout pointed a clawed hand at the ex-hero. 'You? This is turning out to be a great day. I'm gonna kill you too!'

'I thought this might get a little intense. That's why I brought some extra muscle. An old friend of yours, Hunter.'

Chameleon pulled a small remote control out of his pocket and thumbed it. The air on the Sphinx's other paw shimmered, revealing something that had been invisibly cloaked—a huge figure with muscles the size of tree branches bulging under his bodysuit. A metal collar was fixed around his throat, which was the only way Chameleon could control the fiend.

'The Teratoid . . . ' gasped Kirby. That had been one experiment that he didn't want to repeat. The mutation that Scuffer had become was almost as uncontrollable as he was indestructible. Chameleon must be dancing on the edge of madness to have taken him from cryogenics.

'Scuffer?' exclaimed Jake. The Teratoid used to be Warren Feddle, one of Jake's gang before he had betrayed him on a job in Moscow. The last time he had seen Scuffer was in Scotland, and only by a stroke of luck did Jake manage to defeat him then.

'Quite a little reunion of friends, family, and enemies, eh?' smirked Chameleon. 'Hand the pendants over and this can all end quickly and without a fight.'

Jake cracked his knuckles. His face was set in grim determination. The old confidence he had exuded as the school bully was coming back to him. He had nothing to lose.

'Without a fight? Where would the fun be in that?'

Battle Royal

The first attacks came in waves that seemed more pre-planned than the chaotic mess they really were.

Scuffer leapt from the Sphinx's leg and charged at Jake with a roar. He had picked up the scent of his old foe, and didn't need the command to kill. He bulldozed his way through an ancient wall to get at Jake—massive stone slabs spinning in every direction.

Upon sighting Chameleon, Fallout momentarily forgot that his primary orders were to eliminate Jake and retrieve the pendants. Chameleon had been a thorn in his side for many years, and as soon as Scuffer charged for Jake, the villain saw his opportunity to strike at Chameleon.

Pete and Emily hesitated. After Emily had quantum tunnelled in to rescue Pete from events at the Forge HQ, she had persuaded Pete the best course of action was not to fight Jake, but to help him—although Pete was extremely reluctant to do this. Emily had convinced him that, even if Jake still didn't have his powers, he was still Pete's best hope of removing the illness inside him. They had to do whatever it took to get Jake on their side. The appearance of Eric Kirby had persuaded Emily that they were doing the right thing; she was still a downloading hero and proud of it.

What made them hesitate was the noise of multiple explosions around them as Enforcers, heroes, and villains—who had all unexpectedly turned up at the same time—fought amongst themselves.

There was fighting in *every* direction.

Kirby and Orsina both leapt for Chameleon at the same time leaving Jake alone to take the full brunt of Scuffer's initial attack.

Another massive wall collapsed in front of Jake, as his old friend powered through. A shield formed on Jake's arm, so he was able to bat the stone blocks aside—but the weight of it sent him sprawling backwards. Before he could recover, the Teratoid was on him, pinning him to a wall. Scuffer roared like a lion, spittle and bad breath washing over Jake.

'Scuff . . . mate . . . don't you freaks clean your teeth?'

Jake instantly regretted the jibe—he should have been ready to defend himself. Scuffer shoved Jake so hard that they both fell through the thick stone wall.

Chameleon didn't know who hit him first.

Battle Royal

Fallout bounded through the air in a single leap, landing next to the shape-changer. A pointed staff materialized in the villain's hand and he swung it through the air in a series of twists and direction changes that beat the eye. The staff tips glowed as radiation surged through it, causing the air to sizzle as it missed Chameleon's nose by millimetres.

Chameleon backpedalled—only to find his way blocked by Kirby and Orsina.

'This is a little unfair.'

Kirby drew his sword. 'You shouldn't have betrayed the Foundation, then.'

Kirby swung his sword—Chameleon ducked—and the blade clanged with Fallout's staff that was swinging towards Chameleon's head. There was an explosion as the two weapons clashed.

Chameleon was prepared. He pulled out a pair of nunchucks from the recesses of his coat and flung them around with fierce speed—blocking both assaults.

Orsina watched in awe as the three-way fight erupted on the Sphinx's leg. Chameleon was trapped between the hero and villain. Out of the corner of her eye, she caught movement and saw Beth take to the air to save Chameleon.

Orsina couldn't fly, but she wasn't helpless. She ran

and leapt as fast as she could—soaring through the air on a perfect intercept—

She grabbed Beth around the waist and plucked her off course. They both impacted into the statue's chest and dropped into the sands.

Jake groaned as he fell flat on his back. There were only so many walls he could be pushed through before he was worn out. Scuffer wasn't even out of breath.

'Do we have to do this now?' wheezed Jake as dust clouded the air from more toppling rubble.

Scuffer didn't understand. The only thought in his tiny brain was to kill his enemy. Scuffer effortlessly picked up a massive stone block weighing over five tonnes. He hoisted it over his head and bellowed.

Jake raised his feeble energy shield. He doubted it was sufficient protection against the crushing force he was about to receive.

The Teratoid hurled the stone block down with such immense force that it split in two. Scuffer's dull senses realized that there was something wrong when he didn't pick up the scent of blood. His victim should have been pounded into slime.

The dust cleared revealing somebody else leaning over Hunter. Somebody who had risked their life to protect him.

Battle Royal

Jake blinked in surprised at his saviour. 'What . . . ?' was all he could manage.

It was Pete.

The huge rock hadn't hurt him—in fact his body had absorbed the energy of the impact and swollen to over three times its size. Muscles inflated under his cracked cyan skin. He was now an equal match for Scuffer—and a whole lot angrier as memories of how Scuffer had helped Jake bully him at school came flooding back.

'If anyone's gonna pound Hunter apart, it's going to be me—not you!'

Jake scrambled away. Scuffer ignored Pete, and attempted to follow Jake—but was stopped when Pete grabbed his ankle.

'You're not going anywhere, mate!' growled Pete.

Jake watched in astonishment as Pete spun Scuffer around his head like an Olympic hammer thrower. He released him. Scuffer sailed through the air, completely out of control. They all watched as the brute slammed into the side of the Pyramid of Khufu, shattering stone blocks and causing a mini avalanche down the slope. Pete bounded after him.

Jake stood up, still baffled by Pete's sudden alliance. He looked around for Kirby—right now, he was the most important person in the fight. Jake needed that fifth pendant from him.

* * *

Orsina was hurting all over as she tried to stand. Beth picked her off the floor and pinned her to the side of the Sphinx. Her stumped arm suddenly glowed brightly and a translucent hand formed, made from pure energy. Orsina could feel the intense heat even before Beth had shoved it close to her face.

'I am the Reaper,' growled Beth. 'And if you're fighting with the Dark Hunter then you've picked the wrong side!'

Orsina tried to pull Beth's arm away, but it was like hitting metal.

'I know who you are!' cried Orsina in desperation. 'Beth *Hunter* . . . Jake *Hunter*. Same name! He's your brother!'

'Lies!'

'Why do you think you don't see your parents any more?'

Beth hesitated, her glowing hand centimetres from Orsina's face. Orsina could feel the heat burning her cheeks. 'They think you're as bad as Jake. He told me. The Foundation has brainwashed you—'

'Enough!' roared Beth. 'Your time is up!'

Chameleon leapt over a leg sweep from Fallout's staff,

and his nunchucks blocked a decapitating blow from Kirby. The attacks were fast and unrelenting and Chameleon was beginning to tire. He hadn't expected a mass riot with everybody Jake had ever annoyed in the world.

He booted Fallout in the chest. The villain reeled backwards, buying Chameleon enough time to morph into his more dexterous lizard form. He then somersaulted over Kirby's head as the old man lunged forward—

Kirby couldn't stop his attack—the blade missed Chameleon and hit Fallout straight in the chest. The ceramic armour deflected the blade in a shower of sparks.

Fallout roared in fury—his entire black armour suddenly glowing bright green as he charged it with his radioactive power.

Chameleon spun twice through the air—making a perfect landing on the Sphinx's chest. He had to drop his weapon so his claws could find purchase on the rock. He hung, inverted, and watched as Fallout and Kirby battled one another.

Kirby sidestepped Fallout's glowing staff. The impact caused an explosion between the now radioactive staff and the statue. Kirby tried to sidestep the reverse thrust—but the staff struck him across the face.

Chameleon lost count of how many times Kirby pirouetted through the air as he fell off the statue's leg. He was so entertained by the spectacle that he didn't see Fallout point his staff towards him and fire a thick green streamer of radioactive energy.

Orsina's skin burned as Beth's hand hovered milli-metres away—but they both collapsed to the ground as Eric Kirby dropped onto them both. It was a tangle of limbs as they tried to stand—all three suddenly looking up to see Fallout's radioactive blast strike the Sphinx, just above Chameleon.

The ancient neck was severed, and the Sphinx's head rocked, stone grinding on stone before it fell.

Kirby, Orsina, and Beth could only watch in horror as the colossal stone head dropped straight on them.

'Beth!' screamed Jake as he raced towards the Sphinx.

The head crashed against the outstretched forelegs with such force that a huge plume of sand rose up, obscuring the scene.

Fallout hadn't anticipated such destruction. The Sphinx's unusually small proportioned head rolled for-wards, pinning him down under its crushing weight.

Battle Royal

Jake didn't stop running. He gagged on the dust as it filled his lungs and stung his eyes.

A breeze helped clear the cloud a little—and he saw that the head now rested on the front two legs. Kirby, Orsina, and Beth were safely in the hollow between the legs. They looked amazed to be alive.

Jake felt a wave of relief.

Beth saw him—and raised her glowing hand. The energy hand shot forward, trailing a glowing plasma rope that stayed connected to her. The energy fist clobbered Jake with tremendous force. The heat seared the skin off his cheek, burning through to the muscle and bone beneath.

Jake screamed, dropping to the sand. Having his face torn off was starting to be a regular occurrence, and his healing power was already fixing the injury, but it still hurt.

Beth raced over to finish the job.

'This is for my parents,' she snarled.

'Reaper! Wait!' Kirby ran after her. 'Don't hurt him.'

Beth hesitated. Until a few minutes ago she had trusted Eric Kirby implicitly, but now Chameleon had confused the situation by calling him a traitor. She didn't know who to believe.

'Reaper . . . Beth . . . Jake really is your brother. We made you, Chameleon and I. We erased your memory to use you as a weapon to bring the Dark Hunter in.'

Tears welled in Beth's eyes. She looked between Hunter, who was still a stranger to her, and Kirby, the man she had trusted. 'Why?'

'It was a mistake. I see that now. I have made . . . errors of judgement at the Foundation and now they are all coming back to haunt me.' He gave Jake a look heavy with meaning. 'It's time other people did the right thing instead of me.'

'I don't believe you. Chameleon called you a traitor!'

'I can't restore your memory. The only one who could do that is dead now. Your brother will tell you that. He used the last of that hero's power on your parents. Beth . . . you must believe me.'

Pete landed next to Scuffer on the pyramid's flank, and almost slipped off as the stone crumbled beneath his feet.

Scuffer swung at Pete, but missed, pummelling the surface to small debris with the single punch.

An Enforcer chopper circled around, a pair of troopers hanging from the doorway. They had rocket launchers over their shoulders and didn't hesitate to open fire the moment they had the shot.

Pete was expecting missiles to strike them—not the wide nets that enveloped both giants.

'Gah! You idiots!' shouted Pete. 'I'm trying to help!'

He didn't think it was wise to add that he was trying to help a notorious villain.

Both Scuffer and Pete became entangled in their separate nets and slid down the side of the pyramid. By the time they hit the bottom, Pete saw the head of the Sphinx blow off. He saw the tiny speck of Chameleon flying away just in time.

'Wow!'

The distraction got him a punch to the stomach from Scuffer. The Herculean winding was exactly what Pete needed. The energy from the impact traversed through his body, causing him to grow even larger. The net wasn't designed for such strains and ripped apart.

The chopper was hovering low over them, kicking up sand. Pete had had enough. He leapt vertically, high enough to grab the helicopter's tail. The machine couldn't support the sudden weight and lurched down with him.

Before the pilot could recover, Pete grabbed the chopper's tail with both hands, careful to keep the whirling rotor blades away from him, as he swung it around—

He swatted Scuffer as hard as he could with the helicopter. The blades snapped on impact with the Teratoid's impenetrable skin, and the fuselage buckled around him.

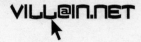

'That's for all those damn wedgies in the school yard!'

'How do I know who to believe?' said Beth in confusion. She looked between Jake and Kirby.

Orsina was the only one who was not focused on the family drama. She was all too aware of the danger around them. She could see that Fallout wasn't moving, slumped under the Sphinx's head. That was one less opponent to worry about. Then she saw Chameleon land on the severed neck of the Sphinx. The huge full moon was framed dramatically behind him, now tinged blood red from the mass of dust kicked in the air from the battles unfolding around them.

'Such a touching family reunion!'

Beth glared at him. 'So it's true?'

'Beth Hunter; Jake Hunter . . . and I thought you would have been bright enough to work that out. You even look the same, you moron! That doesn't matter. Look around, hell has come into town.'

He gestured like a ringmaster and everybody looked. The various battles that had started around them were drawing to a close and the surviving good guys and super-criminals were drawing nearer. A trio of middle-aged Downloaders led the pack, their clothes scorched and bloodied.

Battle Royal

'Oi! You're the Dark Hunter aren't you?' shouted the leader.

'Yeah, I recognize him from the Council canteen. Never sat at our table, the snob.'

The lead goon smirked. 'You got a strong power that a little boy like you shouldn't have. Better give it to me, or else.'

'OK. You can have it.'

Jake raised his hand—and fired a radioactive streamer that sent the leader spiralling into the ruins. The other two reacted in surprise at the ferocity of the attack.

One suddenly caught fire as Chameleon hurled a fireball at him. The other suffered a violent plasma blast from Beth's stump.

'You see,' quipped Chameleon. 'We could be fighting these imbeciles all day. We should just get this over with, and say I won.'

More fortune seekers were drawing nearer. Jake was exhausted and Kirby looked worse for wear. The injury he had sustained from Fallout wasn't healing and his face still bled heavily.

They might be able to beat Chameleon, but they were unlikely to defeat the weaker masses, and with the Enforcer's power dampeners still working around the combat zone, there was little chance of walking away.

Jake noticed Beth was staring at him.

'You really are my brother?' She nursed her stump. 'My own brother did this to me?'

Jake sighed. Same old Beth, worrying about the wrong things at completely the wrong time.

'You were trying to kill me,' he pointed out. 'And it was an accident.'

'Give me what's mine!' shouted Chameleon impatiently.

Emily landed next to Pete as he fought two hero-types who were determined to bring him back to the Foundation for questioning. Lasers pulsed from his eyes, knocking the two do-gooders out.

Emily watched them writhe on the floor in their own world of pain. She felt sorry for them.

'This is madness,' she said.

'It's just one thing after another,' said Pete, watching a group of villains bouncing across the sand in dune buggies; blasting lightning bolts at everybody they passed.

'We have to put the Enforcer dampeners out of action. They're just keeping everybody here and forcing them to fight. We need to give Jake a chance to get away and put things right.'

Pete sighed. 'That sounds so wrong.'

'Pete . . . you promised. And even Kirby is helping him.'

Battle Royal

Pete sighed and nodded. 'OK. Let's go beat up some Enforcers.'

'You lied to me!' Beth shouted at Chameleon. 'You used me!'

Chameleon's tail twitched. 'Get over it,' he shouted back.

Beth shot a venomous look at Kirby. 'And you. I trusted you.'

Kirby wanted to say he was sorry—but Beth suddenly flew up towards Chameleon as fast as she could. Twin pulses of energy shot from her arms, exploding around Chameleon's feet. He hopped aside—then tried to fly away, but a well-aimed blast from Jake caught him in the chest.

Chameleon landed on the Sphinx's outstretched leg, next to Fallout. He groaned in pain; Jake's shot had broken his rib.

Beth landed on the Sphinx's severed head, and looked down on the lizard.

'What you made me do . . . is villainous.'

'Sometimes you have to do bad things to get the right outcome,' retorted Chameleon.

Beth's phantom hand blazed to life. Chameleon shifted back to his human form. He looked pale and coughed 'Look . . . I surrender. Please . . . '

Beth hesitated and dropped down to his level.

Jake frowned. From his vantage point he couldn't fully see Chameleon on the ledge above him. 'Beth, no!'

Beth's hesitation was all Chameleon needed. He shot a fireball at her at point-blank range.

She screamed, falling off the Sphinx and landing hard on the floor. Jake was foaming with anger and apported next to Chameleon.

'You little—'

Chameleon moved too quickly. He snatched Fallout's staff from the villain's dead hand and whirled it around his head. As the staff sliced through the air, it glowed a vibrant green. Chameleon struck the Sphinx's head as hard as he could.

The resulting collision with Fallout's staff was like a pocket-sized nuclear bomb detonating.

The stone head shattered in the explosion. Chameleon and Jake were carried a hundred metres, crashing in to more ruins.

The head broke apart and collapsed on Beth.

Kirby sprang forward, showing agility that belied his years. He managed to grab Beth around the waist to yank her away.

But it was too late.

Tons of broken stone collapsed on them.

With his ears ringing, Jake could feel the change. His

teleportation and jump powers had come back—the dampeners had been destroyed. Pete and Emily suddenly appeared to report the good news . . . but remained silent when they saw Beth's and Eric Kirby's bodies poking from the rubble, twisted and bloodied.

Jake could only stare. His sister was dead.

A cackling laughter drifted over from Chameleon, who was pulling himself from the ruins. He was badly burnt from the explosion. He stopped laughing when he saw what he had done.

Jake felt numb. The moment his sister had accepted who he was, Chameleon had killed her. Kirby's cane lay to one side, the pendant held on the tip. Jake snatched it up, his super-strength crushing the glass orb.

He didn't look at Pete, Emily, and Orsina, all standing around him, unsure what to do.

'You better go,' Jake muttered darkly. Once he had the pendant extracted he looked up and met Pete's eye. Nothing needed to be said between them, and Pete knew it wasn't the right time to ask Jake to remove the virus inside him.

Pete and Emily took to the air and headed towards downtown Cairo. Orsina nodded and teleported away.

Jake pulled the pendants out of his pocket and attached them. He didn't need to fiddle with the pieces as the assembly order was burnt into his memory. They slotted together effortlessly.

The pendant wand pulsed orange and felt different from the last time he used it. Jake could feel the Core Power welling up in his hand.

'You killed my sister.' It was a cold statement.

Chameleon held up his hands, 'It was an accident.'

Jake bellowed, tears suddenly filling his eyes. He pointed the wand at the floor, with no clear idea what he was doing, but the Core Power seemed to have a mind of its own.

A gravity wave spread out from his feet. Sand rippled like water as the wave extended faster than the speed of sound. The weaker ruins trembled and collapsed from the shock wave. The pyramids quivered, the apex of Khafre broke apart and collapsed, shortening the pyramid's height by several metres.

The gravity wave built up to a wall—slamming into the circling Supers and Enforcers with a crushing force. Vehicles were destroyed and people flung with such force that some landed miles away.

A massive cloud of dust rose over the scene of death and destruction—and still Jake Hunter screamed at the loss of his sister.

He raised the pendant, intending to open a black hole within Chameleon's own body . . . but the cowardly killer had teleported the moment Jake had looked away.

Jake just caught sight of the moon as the new dust

pall obscured it. That brought him to his senses. He snapped the pendants apart and tucked them in his pocket. Then turned to the bodies of Kirby and his sister.

One of his greatest enemies had died trying to save his sister and undo a terrible mistake. Jake felt no hatred towards Kirby any more. The old man had given his life to help him.

Now Jake intended to finish things off.

That meant destroying Necros.

Then he would tear the world apart to find Chameleon so he could unleash his full fury.

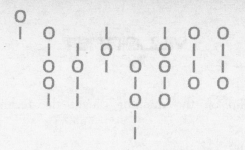

The Library

Deep in the NORAD bunker, the anxious general had long dismissed the notion of going to the barbecue he had planned. Most of the western world was out of power, while the rest of the planet struggled under the yoke of impending moon-fall.

The latest data now showed that the moon was on a firm trajectory that made it increasingly visible over just one part of the sky. In a couple of hours the moon would no longer be visible to the west, and would permanently hang over Asia.

Technician Campbell was still at his post, sweating profusely from the stress of it all. His latest calculations showed that the moon would impact in the Pacific Ocean. There was no danger of a cataclysmic tidal wave because the impact would cause the ocean to vaporize in seconds, before it clove the earth in two.

Every instrument they had and every weapon system that was in place was useless. The general thought that he shouldn't have cancelled the barbecue, it would have made zero difference to the inevitable outcome.

A blip on the monitor caught the technician's eye.

'Oh no . . .'

The general spun on his heels. 'Oh no what? This situation can't go down the pan any quicker than it is doing already.'

The technician tapped a spread of red dots on the screen that hadn't been there earlier.

'We have multiple inbound targets ahead of the moon.'

'What kind of targets?'

'It appears that a field of meteors has been slingshot by the black hole's gravitational pull. They're heading straight for us.'

'Meteors hit the earth all the time.'

'Sure. And a single one supposedly wiped out the dinosaurs. The good news is, if one of these is big enough . . . then we won't be around to watch the moon collide.'

'We must have some missiles to deflect them?'

'No sir. Every military asset is off-line. The only things we have control of is NORAD itself. We're completely on our own.'

Night skies around the world were illuminated by a fantastic display of shooting stars as thousands of meteors burned up in the atmosphere. Streaks of fire shot through the heavens like fireworks.

A few meteors survived and crashed to earth in blazing fireballs, but the resulting clumps of iron were no bigger than a penny—although several impacts smashed windows, crashed through ceilings and, in two instances, ploughed through the bonnets of parked cars.

Because the swarm of meteorites was so huge, the larger ones were packed too close together and collided with one another in the upper atmosphere, thus preventing a fatal attack.

The amazing display lasted for hours, but there were few people to witness it as they were all locked inside their homes, fearing for their lives.

And that was only the first wave.

Jake returned home, but found his parents had gone and the entire town was under a layer of fine dust—the handiwork of a villain called NanoMite that the heroes were dealing with. His parents had left him a note saying they had left town, heading for the countryside where his uncle lived.

Jake didn't see the point in following them. They were probably safe, and he didn't want to be the one who broke the news about his sister.

He had never really got on with Beth as they grew up. When they were both much younger they had laughed and joked together as siblings do, but as they became teenagers, their interests drifted apart and they had very little common ground left. Beth went to a private school and was a star pupil; Jake went to an ordinary school and was a problem child.

He still couldn't bring himself to cry, not properly. A few tears had rolled down his cheek, but otherwise he had been filled with nervous energy and had restlessly paced the house preparing himself for the final confrontation with Necros.

He slapped his face, the sharp pain forcing him to focus. He had no idea how much time he had left to stop the impact, so couldn't afford to waste any. He had five out of the six pendants—and the final one lay around the neck of the fiercest supervillain of them all.

And he had to do it on his own—ironic since he had just been surrounded by people who used to be his enemies, all fighting together for the same goal.

The sudden thoughts of loneliness made him think of his sister again. He couldn't let himself be weak.

'Jake?'

Jake jumped at the sound of his name. He whirled around to see Orsina standing in the living room doorway.

'Oh, it's you,' he mumbled, although he was happy to have company.

Orsina didn't look him in the eye, she felt awkward talking to him.

'I'm . . . sorry about your . . .'

Jake waved her into silence. He had been to a family funeral before when his gran had died and had been baffled by why everybody said 'sorry', as if they were responsible for what had happened. It was something he didn't want to hear.

'I think I can help you with Necros.'

Although having a sidekick would be useful, Jake couldn't bring himself to ask her to fight Necros. It was highly probable that she would die.

'Thanks, but—'

'Hear me out. We don't have time to argue. The moment I left Cairo I tried to round up the others. Pete and Emily ran into more trouble and they're back at the Foundation hospital. Chameleon . . . nobody knows where he is.'

'So that leaves just us.'

Orsina shifted uncomfortably. 'Not quite. There's somebody else you should talk to.'

She stood to one side—revealing Lorna.

Jake scowled. Electrical sparks snapped from his fingers. He was ready to attack.

'Just give me one reason—'

'It wasn't me!' said Lorna. 'Chameleon locked me away and pretended to be me.'

Jake was still suspicious, until Orsina nodded and filled him in on Lorna's captivity.

Jake had mixed feelings. The overriding wave of relief that Lorna hadn't betrayed him was tempered by the fact Orsina had kept it quiet. He would never understand how girls worked.

Jake calmed down and managed to smile at Lorna. 'So you really didn't betray me?'

'Of course not.'

In a movie, this would be the part where he hugged Lorna. But Jake wasn't feeling in the mood. It was enough that she wasn't one of the bad guys after all.

Lorna shouldered past Orsina; the animosity between the two crackled in the air.

'In fact, I've been doing some research that will help you a lot. Proper research with books in libraries, not surfing the net to see what people are blogging about.'

'Tell me.'

'I should show you.'

Jake sighed. He was never one for libraries. 'Lorn . . . I don't have the time to—'

'You better make time. The three of us don't stand a chance against Necros. Even Eric Kirby wouldn't have stood a chance without the might of Hero.com behind him. So your choices are, make time to listen to me, or walk into the Council and give the pendants to Necros. Sure, he'll stop the cataclysm, but without Kirby running the Foundation, the Inner Circle won't be able to stop him from twisting the world to his own dark vision. So, what will it be?'

Jake was expecting the musty smell of collected books. Lorna had quantum tunnelled the three of them into the Reading Room of the Library of Congress in Washington DC.

The massive multi-level circular room amplified the tiniest noise. Lorna nudged him in the ribs and shushed him—her own noise echoing eerily through the large chamber.

The lights were out. The only illumination came from the semi-circular windows high above, and with no moon or streetlights working, it provided very little light.

Lorna had warned them that they couldn't risk venturing outside as running into the supervillain NanoMite would just add unnecessary complication to their mission, and every second counted. She had ensured she and Jake had downloaded nightvision. Orsina hung back, refusing to download any powers, as she was a Prime and had seen the effects of Chameleon downloading powers—it was driving him mad. She stayed at the librarian's central desk while Lorna led Jake to one of the many branching alcoves around the room.

'Orsina gave me the information Forge had hacked from the Foundation's secure servers. It appears that Leech was not the victim he claimed to be. He was a collector, specifically of Core Powers. That's why he was expelled from the Foundation. He was considered dangerous, so Kirby took Leech's son into foster care, only handing him to the Council when he discovered the boy had the same crazy thoughts as his father,' whispered Lorna. There was no guard on duty; in fact the entire city was locked down, so they were in no immediate danger. Whispering just seemed the appropriate thing to do in the grand library.

'So Leech was a bad guy?'

'Not exactly. Misguided, corrupted by power. The online records show that he was looking for a Core Power more powerful than the gravity one.'

A shudder ran down Jake's spine. What exactly had Leech led him into? Lorna continued:

'In the footnotes of the report, it mentioned some very old books. I traced them here. I hid them somewhere I could find them again, and nobody else would look.'

'Why didn't you just take them out?' asked Jake. 'It would have saved time.'

'Because I don't want to keep breaking the rules! No

matter what you think, I'm supposed to be one of the good guys! The only reason there are some one hundred and eighty-eight million books, maps, leaflets, whatever, in these three buildings is because you can't take them out unless you are a high ranking Government employee, like a senator, or a law maker. It's a reference library and it has some amazing things tucked away most people would overlook . . . unless you knew precisely what you were looking for.'

She carefully pulled a pile of books from a shelf and reached to the back, extracting a heavy tome she had hidden there. The cover was made from cracked leather. Faded gold leaf writing revealed the title: *ODDITIES AND UNUSUAL TRAVELS.*

'Here we go,' she said, delicately resting the book on a table and opening the cover with both hands.

'I bet this is all on the internet,' said Jake. 'Everything is.'

'That's quite sad you say that,' said Lorna as she carefully turned the heavy pages. 'The internet's got billions of web pages, but how much of that is copied from somewhere else? It's easy enough to write something incorrect and see it being used by everyone else as a fact.' She giggled. 'That's funny when people do that and you hear about those kids who copied answers from the net and used them in exams—only to find out it was all wrong. That's sad.'

Jake remained tight-lipped. He had done exactly that. Rather than revise for exams, he had printed a few pages off the internet and memorized them. He had taken great pride in being the first in his year to finish the exam, and that was even after he checked through twice so it didn't look as though he was cheating.

He had been more shocked than his parents to discover he had obtained the lowest grades of the year.

'Will you two hurry?' hissed Orsina, her voice echoing across the library as she kept watch.

'Here we go. Look.' Lorna angled the ageing yellow page towards him.

It appeared to be an account of a first mate who was on board a ship caught in a storm in 1846. They had discovered a chain of islands in the Pacific Ocean. It was difficult to read the old spellings, but as far as he could tell, the chronicler spoke of the captain turning into a sorcerer who killed most of his crew then raised the dead to protect the islands. The captain became lord of the island that gave him power over life and death. Jake laughed when he read the name of the author.

'Brier Icky? What kind of stupid name is that?'

'An old one. Besides, Brier's a nice name.'

'Why do I think this is a giant waste of my time?' said Jake irritably. He found the cavernous library spookily like the museum.

The Library

Lorna was feeling unappreciated, so snapped back. 'Maybe because you are an idiot! Keep reading.'

Jake didn't argue. Lorna was the only person who could get away with being so blunt with him. He read through to the end, but was still none the wiser. He shrugged helplessly.

'None of that sounds familiar?'

'It's about a wizard on an island, fighting some mad pirates.'

'Whose power comes from a star found on an island and then hidden in the caves beneath. Didn't you read that part? Does none of it ring any bells? He's talking about Necros!'

'Necros' echoed through the library. Jake read through again. It made some sense: the chain of islands matched the Council's location. He wasn't certain what Necros's powers were, but raising the dead seemed to fit.

'But there are a lot of things wrong. This was written in 1846. How old do you think Necros is?'

'Eric Kirby is much older than he looks. Looked,' she corrected herself. 'There's something about their powers that make them last longer than normal people. Back then, superpowers would look exactly like magic powers. That's why Necros built the Council of Evil there. He built it on the source of all his power. How many times have you ever seen or heard of him leaving the island?'

'A few. He does do it . . . not very often though.'

'But he gets everybody else to do his dirty work for him. According to the text he draws his powers from whatever is in the cave. Perhaps when he leaves the island he can only do so for a short while, or he's weaker.' Lorna turned the page and pointed to another paragraph. 'This tells of how the chronicler escaped by severing the sorcerer's connection with his power source. It made him weak and vulnerable. That's what you need to do if you're going to beat him.'

Jake ran through the possibilities as Orsina joined them; she was fed up with only hearing bits of the conversation.

'You think this guy is Necros? If he draws powers from under the island does that make him a Prime or what? Could that be that he has another Core Power?'

Jake was thinking hard. 'Maybe, or maybe he downloads them too, but rather than digitally, through a more basic set up. Like radio waves or something. He gets his powers from being close to their source.'

'Whatever's under there gives him his strength. So, theoretically, we should be able to use it to weaken him. What are his powers anyway?'

Jake looked blank. Every Prime had their main ability, like Orsina's super-speed, and some, like her, had less powerful secondary powers. Stronger Primes, like the Council members, usually possessed a terrifying array of powers. But Necros was just known for being a formidable opponent. Jake couldn't recall any tales describing his powers.

Orsina suddenly looked up into the darkness. She had heard something.

'Somebody's in here,' she whispered. 'They've found us.'

They ducked behind the shelves, then peeked down the dark aisle. A glimmer of light hovered in the air: it was an open portal. Beyond the portal they could see daylight, and a room laid out with electronic equipment. Some technicians were visible in jeans and T-shirts with the Forge logo.

Jake tensed when he recognized the figure through the portal.

It was Chameleon. He peered into the dark library and allowed two other Forge members to step through. They were huge men, built like professional wrestlers. The leader carried a heavy-duty gun of a design Jake had never seen before. A cylinder, the diameter of an old record, was mounted over an unusual wide barrel.

Both Lorna and Orsina gripped Jake's arms and shook their heads as anger took over reason.

'He's going down,' growled Jake.

'Not yet. Jake . . . you can't waste time on him until you stop the collision course. Think about it.'

As much as Jake wanted to fire every superpower he

had downloaded at Chameleon's grinning face, he forced himself not to.

'The portal is stable,' declared a technician from the room beyond. 'The trace works.'

The scientists in the background clapped and cheered their achievement until Chameleon silenced them.

'Shut up, fools. They can hear you through there.' He addressed the two goons. 'Gort, Hammer. Begin your recce. Hunter tunnelled through here not so long ago. We should be able to pick up the quantum flux if he has moved on.'

Orsina whispered. 'They got the tunnel detector to work! Forge scientists stole it from the Council of Evil. Since quantum tunnelling was almost undetectable, they wanted to find a way to detect and re-open portals so they could chase people through them.'

'Then that's no longer a safe way to travel,' said Lorna.

'Not unless you want Forge on your tail. That place was . . . is our research lab away from the main head-quarters. I'm guessing that's the only part of Forge still up and running.'

Gort and Hammer spread out along the concentric aisles. They walked with confidence, which meant they had nightvision powers too.

'So what do we do?' whispered Lorna.

They both looked at Jake. He pulled out his phone.

The Library

'Since none of us bothered downloading teleport, I think I better do it and get out of here.'

He accessed Villain.net. Immediately a small device on Gort's arm PINGED for attention.

'He's here! Pickin' up cellphone activity!' He pivoted around until he was facing Jake's hiding place. 'Right there!'

He fired his rifle. Spinning discs shot from the gun. They resembled circular buzz-saw blades and moved like bullets. The round blades chewed effortlessly through the books and shelves—nicking Jake's ear.

Jake blasted a radioactive volley. The energy arced out and struck Gort who was lifted into a bookcase. Pages fluttered in the air, some catching fire from the extreme heat.

Lorna shoved Jake's arms aside.

'Stop it! You'll destroy the library! It was bad enough with the museum and the Great Wall. Try and do something less destructive!'

Her interference gave Gort a chance to roll aside and pat out his smouldering T-shirt.

Hammer swung a punch—his arms extended a dozen metres, his fists forming massive sledgehammers that obliterated the bookcase shielding Jake.

Lorna got caught by a backstroke of the hammer fist and was thrown into the reading room, crashing in the darkness.

Jake thrust his fingers into his attacker's retreating arm and delivered a powerful electric shock. Hammer screamed as the voltage coursed through his system.

Jake leapt to his feet since his hiding place had been destroyed. He had a perfect shot across the library at Chameleon framed in the glowing portal. Jake switched powers and pointed at Chameleon.

'Close the portal!' Chameleon screamed at the technicians. 'Hurry!'

Jake felt raw energy surge through his body, but he restrained himself from firing. His hands throbbed painfully as they acted like stoppers in a bottle, desperate to be freed.

Just as Jake thought he was going to burst from the energy building inside him, he let loose the solid blue beam from his index finger.

The energy was colossal and finely focused from one finger. Jake's aim was perfect—but the Forge scientists managed to pull the plug in time. The portal snapped shut as the beam was about to hit Chameleon. It shot across to the other side of the library and blasted a massive hole through the wall, into the courtyard beyond.

'Jake!' wailed Lorna's disapproving voice through the darkness. 'What did I tell you?'

'It was an accident!'

Gort had found his feet again and fired multiple discs at Jake. The circular blades dashed through several bookcases. Jake sprinted for cover—one blade embedding into the stone above his head.

If Lorna was going to give him earache for damaging the library, what could he use against his two attackers?

'Get us out of here,' shouted Orsina.

Jake's hand went for his mobile—it had fallen from his pocket and was lying across the chamber, the screen still glowing.

'Rats!'

He took a deep breath and ran for the phone. Gort's shots sliced the ground behind Jake, the sharp discs bouncing off the stone floor like skipping stones across a lake.

Orsina suddenly appeared next to Gort and slugged him across the face with the heaviest book she could find. Several of the thug's teeth dropped out and he collapsed on the floor.

Jake reached out for his phone—just as a sledgehammer fist smashed it apart, the tiles cracking from the impact.

'You ain't going nowhere, boy!' laughed Hammer.

Jake's radioactive power dripped from his hands. His temper snapped and he didn't care what damage he caused in the library—

Hammer's arms snapped back to normal size, but still resembled hammers. He drew back for a punch.

Lorna suddenly appeared from the darkness behind the thug and blew on him. An ice blast flowed from her mouth, freezing Hammer on the spot. Icicles formed from his arm as he was completely encased.

Lorna gave Jake a disapproving look.

'You can't go smashing your way through everything in your path. No matter how angry you are.'

Orsina examined Lorna's handiwork. 'Nice job.'

The compliment made Lorna smile; at least someone appreciated her effort. Jake huffed: typical that the girls were sticking together. He picked up the remains of his mobile. It was unidentifiable. 'Now what do we do?'

'We go to the Council of Evil as planned and end it all.'

'But Chameleon will still be able to track us if we don't teleport,' Jake pointed out. 'I can only tunnel.'

Orsina shrugged. 'We're heading into the heart of darkness. I don't think it matters too much if he wants to join us there.'

Jake looked at them both questioningly. 'Us? I don't want you coming with me. This is way too dangerous. I can't guarantee your safety, especially after what happened to . . .'

The girls approached him, and hooked his arm, one on each side.

'We weren't giving you the option,' said Orsina.

The Library

'We thought we'd come along and guarantee *your* safety, actually.'

Jake couldn't think of a suitable argument. He opened up a portal and stared at his Council Chamber beyond.

'This is it then. The last step.'

He led the way through.

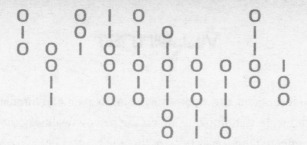

What Lies Beneath

Jake stepped out into his private Council of Evil chamber. The first thing that struck him was the fact that the entire place had been ransacked. Word of his treachery had obviously spread across the island. Jake instantly regretted walking back into his own office: he should have picked somewhere a little more secluded on the island.

Lorna and Orsina followed him in.

'Do you always keep it this tidy?' said Orsina.

'Funny,' snorted Jake as he headed straight for the remains of the storage cabinet. The locked doors had been blown open and the contents thrown onto the floor. He searched through the junk until he found what he needed: several spare mobile phones. He took one and thumbed it on and V-net immediately appeared.

Lorna moved to the door. She could hear a faint whooping alarm from outside. 'What's that noise?'

'I think it's the evacuation alarm,' said Jake, pocketing the phone. 'We should move quickly.'

He opened the door—surprising a pair of Duradan who were standing outside on the narrow walkway that connected his chamber to the mainland. They wore full-body black ceramic armour that sported numerous sharp fins and angular vents that made the soldier look like a cross between a shark and a porcupine. They were the Council's private security that could instantly download whatever powers they needed from the island's Wi-Fi. They were specially trained not to have a sense of humour.

Jake blasted one with a radioactive pulse. Orsina charged the other with her super-speed—the impact caused the guard to stagger over the walkway barrier. He fell a hundred and seventy metres into the crashing waves below.

'Come on!' shouted Jake as he charged across the bridge. The Duradan were only deployed in times of absolute crisis, the Council's last line of defence. Now there were only two Council members left, Necros and Abyssal . . . and Abyssal was not known for his courage. Jake guessed the villain had fled the island as soon as he was able.

It was dark as the trio ran across the bridge towards the main island. They could see bright meteors shooting across the sky with violent fury. Everything was dominated by the moon that now stretched from horizon to horizon. In the distance, fireballs dropped from the sky and hit the ocean in violent explosions.

As they watched, a chunk of meteor streaked down and took out the bridge connecting Chromosome's old private island that lay next to Jake's. The burning bridge collapsed into the raging water below; the sound of twisting metal reverberated over the evacuation alarm.

It felt like the end of the world.

Jake stopped. His legs would no longer carry him. The scene around him was a nightmare, and he could only guess how the rest of the world was suffering. And it was all his fault.

Kirby, his sister . . . dead because of him.

If only he hadn't set events in motion . . .

'Move!' Lorna screamed down his ear as she shoved him towards the door that would take them to the mainland.

Jake broke from his reverie and blasted the door open, knocking out a Duradan standing behind it. Jake jumped through the hole as a second guard opened fire with energy darts firing from his gloved fist.

Jake returned fire, but missed the guard. Lorna tried her freezing breath again, but the Duradan's armour melted the ice. The guard swung a punch at Lorna, holographic spikes forming on his gloved fist. Lorna just managed to sidestep as the spikes solidified and crunched into the wall—momentarily sticking the Duradan's hand in place. He tried to extract the spikes before realizing he could just as easily turn the hologram off—by which time Lorna had booted him so hard he sailed up like a football, crashing into the corridor's low ceiling, where his armoured fins held him in place, unconscious.

'How many more of these guys are there?' asked Lorna with concern.

'Lots. We're going to have to fight through them to get wherever it is we're heading.'

'Down. Whichever corridors lead down.'

Without a clear mental picture of where they were heading it was impossible to teleport or quantum tunnel. That meant there would be a lot of adversaries to fight: Duradan, ambassadors who ran the evil empire, and every have-a-go-villain who lived and worked on the island and was stupid enough to hang around during the apocalypse.

The main body of the island was a vast, multi-level city that housed the Council of Evil's research labs, countless administration offices, and the entire Villain.net server farm and raw powers. It was home to tens of thousands of technicians, engineers, caterers, and administration staff—a whole city devoted to keeping the forces of evil running smoothly and efficiently.

What Lies Beneath

'We can't fight them all,' said Lorna.

The earth shook as a meteor hit close by. The Duradan fell from the ceiling with a clang. Jake nudged the prone guard with his foot.

'I've got an idea,' he said with a smile.

The squad of Duradan jogged down the corridor in formation. The base rumbled as another meteor struck. The lights flickered and the constant siren suddenly choked off. The whole island was plunged into darkness for a couple of seconds before the red emergency lighting illuminated the corridor.

Through a cracked panoramic window, the Duradan squad watched as a mushroom cloud rose from the island's main power station. Luckily the Council of Evil had been very environmentally conscious and had employed solar, wind, and, more importantly, tidal generators on the island. The constant swell of the ocean was more than enough to keep vital systems online such as emergency power, air conditioning, core computer systems, and Villain.net.

A secondary explosion blossomed from the power station, casting debris into the water. Another meteor screamed by, missing the island by half a kilometre.

Although highly trained, the Duradan were still awed by the spectacle, and unaware that other troopers had joined them to gawp out of the window. The Duradan sergeant suddenly became aware that his squad was larger.

'What's going on here?' came his amplified voice through the helmet. He had a distinct Welsh accent. 'Who's not supposed to be in me unit?'

A chorus of voices confirmed they all should be.

'Obviously not!' barked the sergeant. 'There were six of us minutes ago, and now I'm counting nine. Come on, some of you should be with another unit. Who's just joined?'

One trooper suddenly became aware that a finger was pointing at him. He reacted instantly. 'It wasn't me, Sarge!' He turned to his accuser. 'Who're you under there? Is that you, Neil?'

'No, I'm Neil,' said another voice.

'No, I am,' declared another.

The sergeant's patience was wearing thin. That was the trouble with all wearing identical uniforms and helmets, you were never sure who was who. His musings were interrupted by sudden laser blasts from three of the Duradan. The squad hadn't been expecting the attack—and two of them were blasted through the window, which shattered under their weight.

Another was hit by a sonic wave that came from another guard's arm—while two more accidentally shot one another.

What Lies Beneath

One Duradan unfurled a crackling light whip from his sleeve—and a female voice shrieked from his intended victim.

'Jake, no! It's Lorna!'

The whip fizzled in Jake's hand and he pulled off his helmet. He was sweating heavily beneath it. The sergeant recognized him immediately.

'Hunter?'

The third Duradan struck the sergeant with a lightning bolt. He fell against the wall, his armour short-circuiting. Orsina pulled her helmet off and admired her handiwork.

'I love these suits!' Rather than download the powers into the user, the suits handled the powers directly, meaning Orsina could download any power from the server without worrying about side effects. The suits had been a brilliant disguise and they had managed to make it halfway across the city.

Jake unclipped the sergeant's helmet, and tossed it aside. The man inside had a cropped marine haircut, and was drooling from the shock. His eyes rolled, unfocused, and he was lucky to still be alive. Jake gently slapped the man's face to focus him.

'OK, big guy. We need directions.'

'Urrrrgh . . . ' More drool rolled from his lips.

'Focus. Come on. We need to get under the island. There are some caves, right?'

'Uck.'

'Caves. Do you know what's in them?'

The man's eyes started to focus. 'For . . . bidden . . . '

'That sounds like them. Where are they?'

'Forbid . . . '

'Yeah, yeah. I know. How do we get there?'

'Doc . . . '

'I'll get you a doctor if you answer the question.'

'Doc . . . doc . . . '

Jake shook the man roughly, but he fell unconscious.

'Well that didn't help.'

Lorna took off her helmet. 'What if he didn't mean doctor? The caves were found by a sailor. So would they be up here? This high?'

The answer struck Jake. 'The docks... of course. This place gets a regular supply in from boats. I've just never been down there.'

He slid his helmet back on. An HUD appeared over the visor. Like his SkyByke, the onboard computer tracked Jake's eye movement and moved the pointer across the display. Using the optic-interface, Jake opened a 3D map of the island.

'Plot a path to the dock.'

Ordinarily, the chirpy voice of Ernie, the Council's artificially intelligent computer system would narrate directions, but with everything running on emergency power, Ernie's more human functions had been deactivated. Instead, a solid line appeared on the map, showing the quickest route.

'It's eight minutes away. Let's go!'

Waves slammed into the huge wharf that had been constructed across the bay. It was one of the few places where the island didn't meet the ocean with a vertical cliff.

Jake, Lorna, and Orsina left the elevator at a run, but quickly stopped. Even though the bay was sheltered, the waves hammered the concrete quayside. The remains of smaller boats were littered across the wharf, but what alarmed them most was the 120,000 tonne oil tanker that had been lifted from the water and hurled across the dock. One enormous propeller was still turning and they would have run straight into it. It didn't rotate quickly, but had gouged the concrete walkway. The steel structure was on its side and slowly collapsing from its weight, spewing millions of gallons of oil into the bay.

According to Jake's map, a 'Forbidden Zone' lay at the end of the wharf, just beyond the tanker. Jake was unable to fly over the lake of oil that was welling from the fractured hull. The girls took to the air, hooked him under each arm and carried him over the oil slick.

Ahead they could see a huge tarnished steel door built into the side of the cliff face. It was two storeys high, and even in the intense moonlight, it looked impenetrable. Jake's HUD map indicated that the Forbidden Zone lay beyond. They were in luck, ordinarily the wharf and door would have been heavily guarded but the disaster was providing them with the perfect opportunity to break in.

They had just cleared the bridge, some thirty storeys above the spinning propellers, when Jake glanced across the water and saw a fireball crash into mouth of the bay, almost a mile away. The problem was the rough seas had already carried the oil that far.

The oil on the water's surface caught fire, and raced towards them at a phenomenal speed.

'Fly faster!' he yelled.

'This armour's weighing us down!' Lorna snapped back.

The entire bay suddenly erupted in a wall of fire twenty metres tall. The trio were nothing more than specks arcing over the tanker. They cleared the ship and made it halfway to the reinforced door as the flaming sea connected with the huge oil tanker.

Jake doubted any of their powers could protect them from the impending explosion. He did the only thing he could—and opened a quantum portal directly in front of them.

What Lies Beneath

They passed through and closed it with milliseconds to spare.

Jake, Lorna, and Orsina suddenly appeared on a tropical beach. It would have been daylight if the gargantuan moon hadn't been blocking the sun. They dropped on the white sands, the gentle surf lapping around their feet. It was very peaceful.

'Where are we?' asked Orsina.

Lorna looked around and saw the remains of a mansion on the tiny island. It had been battered by a hurricane. Only a few internal walls were left standing.

'This used to be Pete's,' she said.

'Safest place I could think of,' said Jake. 'Now, time to go back.'

He opened another portal and leapt back into the Council's dock.

It was hell on earth.

Everything was on fire. The supertanker had split into several huge chunks during the explosion. One section, about the size of a tower block, was still spinning through the air—crashing against the furthest cliff wall.

Every centimetre of floor and cliff was coated with burning oil. Peering from the portal, Jake thought it was as if they were inside the sun.

'Make yourselves fireproof,' he said as he stepped out.

The Duradan battlesuits absorbed the intense heat as they waded through the fire. Burning oil sloshed around their feet, sticking to the armour so that their legs were aflame. If it hadn't been for the suits' internal oxygen generator, they would have suffocated as the fire sucked the air.

Jake had thought the wildfire in California had been bad. It was a candle compared to the furnace around them.

They pushed towards the steel door, and were glad to see that the explosion had buckled it partially away from the wall. It was three metres thick, and if it hadn't been for the explosion, Jake wondered how they would have managed to get through. Now, all they had to do was squeeze inside.

It was like walking into a wind tunnel. Air was being sucked through the narrow fissure to feed the oil fire outside. The airflow was so intense it immediately extinguished the fires on their legs. All three were forced to lean forwards at an acute angle to the ground in order to walk, using their hands against the wall to propel them forward.

It was pitch black, and they could only see the path ahead with their nightvision. Orsina's visor down-loaded the necessary power so she wasn't blind.

The tunnel angled gently down and eventually opened up into a larger chamber. The intense air flow eased as the space increased. Jake saw lights had been strung across the wall, but they obviously didn't warrant emergency power as they remained dark.

He switched the suit from internal to external oxygen. He was expecting the air to smell stale as they ventured down, but he could detect the strong scent of saltwater.

The tunnel suddenly opened up into a cavern about the size of an aircraft hangar. The floor dropped away a few metres revealing a subterranean saltwater lake. The pathway continued to spiral around the cavern edge, leading to a wooden quay.

What surprised Jake most was the pirate galleon berthed at the jetty.

It was battered. Fragments of the burnt and rotting sails still clung to the charred masts.

'That's . . . not what I thought we'd find,' breathed Lorna.

'It's awesome,' said Jake. As a kid, he had always wanted to grow up and be a pirate. Typically his parents had never approved.

'Just as the book described,' said Lorna as they descended to the quay.

Something Leech had said stirred in the back of Jake's memory. He had once called Necros a pirate. Obviously he knew.

From the jetty they could read the boat's name: *The Buccaneer*. A gangplank led onto the deck.

'That's nuts . . . ' breathed Orsina.

Jake tested his weight on the gangplank. It creaked, but held. 'Think about it. Eighteen . . . whatever, he discovers these islands, and something here gives him his powers. The guy who wrote that book escaped as he massacred the crew . . . '

'Eric Kirby!' exclaimed Lorna. 'Brier Icky, what a stupid name. It's an anagram for Eric Kirby. He was with Necros . . . he must have been a pirate too!' She was shocked by her deduction.

Jake didn't have the mental gymnastics to work out the anagram, so he took Lorna's word for it.

'Kirby was a pirate . . . you know, I always suspected he had a bad streak. So, they were both here. Necros, or whatever his name was back then . . . Sec Nor,' he guessed glibly.

'Crones,' added Orsina with a giggle.

Lorna sighed. It was never easy being smart around dumb people. 'It doesn't mean everybody's an anagram. I reckon Kirby was here with his brother—Leech. He knew about this place too. Something here provides Necros with his power. And I bet it's on the boat.'

Jake ascended on deck. The water was as calm as a millpond and the ship was rock steady. The old wooden planks griped under his feet. Two large hatches were spread across the deck. The sterncastle rose at the back, covered in florid Spanish designs.

'Why would he hide the power here? Why not keep it close? Whatever it is.'

'Perhaps he can't move it. This is a Forbidden Zone. Who comes down here?'

'It wasn't exactly well hidden,' said Jake. 'I mean, the door was in plain sight.'

'According to the map on my HUD, there are radioactive symbols all over this area. I'd say that's enough to keep the most persistent snoop away. Besides, who else suspects Necros is drawing his powers from the island?'

Jake wasn't convinced. 'It could be anywhere down here. We don't have time for a treasure hunt.'

Lorna ran through her options on the HUD. As it was connected to a battery of sensors on the island, she could access almost everything. 'We don't have to waste time looking everywhere. Those goons in the library gave me an idea when they traced your mobile phone signal. We just need to lock onto a Higher Energy signal that isn't us.'

A radar-like map appeared on her HUD. Concentric circles radiated out from her suit at the centre. They highlighted Jake and Orsina's Higher Energy signals radiating through their suits and bodies—and a third target below decks.

'Bingo! Follow me.'

Lorna led them to the hatch closest to the fo'c's'le. Lorna remembered her history lessons. 'The fore-castle was where the crew slept. I bet this is the galley.'

She had to use her super-strength to pull the hatch back. Dust fell from the heavy wood and it slammed against the deck like a tombstone, echoing through the chamber. They waited for the echo to subside before descending the wooden steps.

It was the galley. Long benches were covered with rusting metal plates, knives, and lanterns. A wild assort-ment of fungus now lived on the table, having long ago spawned from the decaying food. The stench was over-powering, making the trio return to their suits' oxygen supply. The stench didn't come from the fungus. It came from the bodies.

A dozen skeletons lay about the cabin. They were over a century old. Several had been pinned to the wall by swords thrust through their chests. Others lay in the position they had fallen when sliced apart by a wicked sword blade. Another's skull lay a metre away. It was carnage. The wood was stained black from the spilled blood.

'Somebody went axe-happy,' whispered Orsina.

'Necros,' stated Jake. 'He killed his crew. I reckon he didn't want anyone else to know his secret.'

What Lies Beneath

Lorna nodded. 'And Kirby escaped to become his arch-enemy.'

'This is creeping me out,' whispered Orsina.

Jake became aware that all the bodies lay as if they had been facing the same direction. He speculated they had been facing Necros at the head of the table, presumably as he opened the chest that still stood there.

'That's where the Higher Energy is coming from,' Lorna confirmed. 'It's in the chest.'

Jake stood in front of the chest. It was no bigger than a shoebox and was covered in naggingly familiar looking ornate carvings. It looked much older than the galleon. A rusted metal clasp held it closed. Inside, lay the source of Necros's power.

And his weakness.

'I guess we open it,' he said nervously.

'Wait,' said Orsina urgently. 'What if the same thing that drove him to kill the rest of the crew . . . is still in there?'

A faint reverberation from another meteor impact shook the cavern. Debris trickled from the ceiling, splashing into the water.

Jake took a deep breath. 'We really don't have time to debate that.'

He opened the chest.

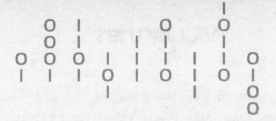

The Last Stand

Jake didn't know what to expect, but he didn't expect a deep sigh to reverberate through the boat, shaking the timbers. He had positioned the chest at an angle, so it opened away from him, just in case anything popped out jack-in-the-box style.

He cautiously peered around. Mist swelled from the box. Inside, he could just make out a dark crystal that glowed deep purple. The crystal seemed to regularly expand and contract like a heart.

'What is it?' asked Lorna.

'It's just a breathing rock,' said Jake. It seemed harmless enough.

Orsina moved closer. She had been taking cover behind a wooden stanchion. 'Try and smash it. If it's linked to Necros we don't want it around.'

Jake pulled one of the swords from the decaying skeleton. It felt heavy as he weighed it in his hand, making a few experimental cuts through the air.

'We don't even know what power it gives him,' Lorna pointed out. 'Maybe we don't have to destroy it?'

Jake hesitated while swinging the sword. He had seen something similar before. Then it came to him.

'Leech had a chest like this one. I saw it back in Tibet. And inside there was something glowing purple like this. Wrapped away.'

'Then Leech and Necros have the same powers?' asked Orsina.

'They're certainly linked,' said Jake. 'He could have stolen it. Lorn, you said he was a collector, right?'

'Yeah. Possibly. But does it matter? Leech is dead and whatever this thing is, I guess we'd be better off without it.'

Jake nodded. He swung the sword down as hard as he could. It hit the crystal with a dull clang and bounced off, rust flaking from the blade. The crystal was unharmed, but he swore it appeared to be beating faster.

Purple streamers suddenly arced from the crystal. They licked across the wooden ceiling like static electricity bursts. The air buzzed loudly as they lashed out, searching for something.

Jake backed away. Lorna was already at the base of the steps, Orsina had super-sped back to the deck.

The purple sparks suddenly struck a skeleton—then all the power seemed to focus on the one set of bones before pinballing around the cabin, striking the other skeletons. The purple lightning curved around Jake and Lorna to reach its dead targets.

The Last Stand

'I've got a bad feeling about this,' Jake muttered.

'Close the lid!' Lorna shouted.

Jake swung at the chest's lid with his sword. It slammed back over the crystal, instantly cutting the lightning off.

'That was weird,' said Orsina. 'Do you think that's what killed the pirates?'

One of the skeletons suddenly bolted upright in front of Jake. It moved fluidly, its bony hand unsheathing its sword. Jake was shocked as the blade whirled close to his head—and he only raised his one sword at the last second to parry the blow.

The other skeletons suddenly leapt into action, removing the blades that had killed them and using them as weapons.

'What's going on?' cried Jake.

He swung his sword, but the skeleton expertly blocked it. Dust fell from the old bones as the skeleton shook from the impact.

Lorna hurled a fireball from her suit—the flames passed through the skeleton opposite her and blew a hole in the wall. The skeleton was unfazed by the attack. It lunged for her as another struck her from behind. The ancient blade snapped against her tough ceramic armour—but she was surrounded by four of the animated skeletons.

Jake parried another thrust and punched the pirate

skeleton in the face. The skull cracked diagonally in half, but the skeleton was unrelenting in its attack.

Orsina ran in and helped Lorna boot her assailants away. Three of the skeletons smashed apart against the interior hull, but the others continued pressing their attack.

Jake panicked and used his own powers rather than the suit's—not the smartest move. A radioactive blast from his hand shattered the armoured glove he was wearing as the blast was forced out.

The skeleton attacking him was torn apart—ribs, femurs, and assorted bones clattering against the wall.

Jake regrouped with Lorna and Orsina, standing back-to-back as the other bone warriors circled around them. The only noise they made was the clatter of bone on wood, which made the hollow skulls appeared scarier.

'This is freaking me out,' said Lorna.

The skeletons they had broken against the walls, started to stir. The bones rolled across the floor, reforming the skeletons. The team watched in astonishment as the skeletons began reassembling.

'We can't kill them,' said Jake.

'They're not alive in the first place,' Lorna pointed out. 'Whatever it is in that box is reanimating them.'

'Or bringing them back alive,' said Orsina ominously.

'That's impossible,' said Lorna.

The Last Stand

'Yes, but so is this,' retorted Orsina as she fired spherical energy pulses from her hand. Two of the skeletons exploded, but almost instantly began to reform.

'They might be unstoppable,' said Jake, 'but we came here to get rid of Necros's main source of power. What's in that chest is keeping him alive.'

'Makes sense.'

'Then we have to get rid of it. Cover me.'

Lorna and Orsina stood in front of Jake and fired shots at the horde. Some passed through their attackers' ribs, damaging support beams or tables below deck. A few lucky shots blasted the skeletons into piles of bones, only for them to quickly reform.

Orsina staggered under numerous sword blows as four skeletons rushed her from the side. Luckily the blades were no match against her armour, and she ran through them, shattering the bones apart like bowling pins. It was a stand-off, with neither side winning.

'Jake, whatever you're doing, do it faster!' shouted Lorna.

Behind them, Jake took off his helmet and threw it at the skeleton captain who was getting too close for comfort. The armoured helmet knocked the captain's head off, and the body blindly fumbled around trying to retrieve it.

Jake pulled his remaining glove off to free his hands

so he could pull a section of his thigh armour off to reach into his pocket. His fingers wrapped around four of the pendants. He was trembling as he tried to fit them together correctly.

'Hurry!' shouted Lorna as the girls fought off another rush attack.

The four sections snapped together. It was the minimum force Jake could use, and he was more than conscious of what could happen. He just hoped Kirby had been correct when he said Jake was beyond being corrupted by power.

The pendant wand glowed in his hand. He closed his eyes, easing his temper. The calmer he was, the more control he could exercise.

'Hold on to something!' he shouted.

He wrapped one arm around a wooden stanchion. Lorna and Orsina immediately understood what he meant and did the same.

Jake pointed the wand at the chest. Black particles shot from the end, a swarm of gravitons. They formed around the chest, orbiting faster and faster as they opened a tiny black hole. Jake was trying to be careful, and concentrated on opening a portal no bigger than a pinhole.

Everything on the table slid towards the black hole, which was sucking the air from the boat. Jake's ears popped from the sudden change in air pressure.

The Last Stand

The ship lurched as the entire structure tried to implode.

The chest started to rock—and then was suddenly plucked into the tiny black hole. Jake couldn't tear his gaze away as the chest crushed in on itself. Debris from around the room flowed in, and Jake was dragged towards the hole. He increased his grip on the stanchion.

The dozen skeletons were dragged across the floor, arms scrambling to hold on to something. Some managed, but their arms were torn off. In seconds, all the skeletons had been sucked into the vortex along with half the ship's fittings.

Jake banished the black hole—junk that was still flying through the air clattered to the floor.

The mysterious chest had gone.

'Well that worked,' said Jake with a smile.

'Where do those things go when they're sucked into a black hole?' asked Orsina.

'I think gravity just tears them apart. Why?'

Orsina looked thoughtful. 'If it brought those skeletons back to life, maybe it could bring other people . . . like his sister?' she whispered to Lorna.

Lorna nudged her in the ribs and gave her a look to silence her. 'Not now!'

Orsina nodded. Jake hadn't guessed anything and the less Jake was distracted the better. Fortunately he hadn't heard their exchange.

'Well, I have no idea if that is going to make Necros any weaker, but I think now is the time to find out. This is where we part.'

Lorna frowned. 'What do you mean? We're coming with you.'

Jake shook his head. 'Too many people have died. I can't have anything happening to you on my conscience.'

Lorna was furious. She put her hands on her hips. 'Jake Hunter, how dare you—'

'Sorry, Lorn. This wasn't a discussion.'

With a loud bang he used a downloaded power to teleport out of the cavern. He knew they couldn't follow him as neither had been in the Council's assembly chamber or even seen pictures of it, so they couldn't envision his destination.

He was ready to face Necros alone for the final showdown.

The very moment Jake appeared, he shot a laser pulse across the chamber. He reasoned whoever was in the chamber must be a foe. The shot exploded in an empty alcove, destroying the seat it held. That had been his own seat.

Jake looked around the dark chamber. Not so long ago he had taken his seat here as a member of the

The Last Stand

Council of Evil. Each alcove held a Council member, the most diabolical supervillains the world had known. Jake had eliminated most of them, with a little help. Only Necros and Abyssal remained, and, true to form, he could see Abyssal's jacuzzi-style throne was vacant. He was always the first to flee when trouble started.

If he hadn't decided to topple the Council of Evil in revenge for how they had used him, he could still be here enjoying power beyond the reach of most mortals, and the moon wouldn't be minutes away from destroying the earth.

But because of events he had set in motion, the building around him trembled as meteors rained fire from above.

'Necros!'

Jake was aware that his nightvision wasn't working. He doubted that it would have expired so soon. He recalled Necros always had the power to be wreathed in shadows. That meant he must be somewhere close. Red emergency lights provided the only illumination.

He became aware of ragged breathing and tracked the source to the arch-villain himself, who was seated on his throne.

'There you are,' growled Jake. He held the pendant wand in his hand, ready to use absolute force if necessary.

'The Dark Hunter . . . ' wheezed Necros. He didn't

sound his usual self. 'You bring destruction wherever
you go.'

'I'm here for the last piece of the pendant, Necros.
Give it to me so we can stop the collision. Then we can
settle things between us.'

Necros laughed, although there was zero humour in
it. 'Then why didn't you simply ask. Maybe then we
could have reached an agreement rather than you sid-
ing with Leech.'

'How did you know about him?'

'You told me yourself. An unfortunate choice of
words when you told me Lorna had leeched your powers. I knew you had been in contact with that collector.'

Jake was puzzled. Why hadn't Necros attacked him?
Time was running out and they couldn't afford the
casual chat they were having. Jake saw the pendant
around Necros's neck and took a step forward.

A hand suddenly swiped the pendant from Necros
and held it up in the dim light. It was Leech. The old
man stepped out, dangling the pendant for Jake to see.
He didn't look so old this time. He was more youthful
than ever.

'The last piece, Jake,' said Leech with a smile. 'We
did it.'

'I thought you'd died in the air strike?'

'Apparently not. Some powers can transcend even
death.'

The Last Stand

'Give me the last piece and we can stop this,' said Jake, although he had already guessed what was coming next.

'Why don't you give me the five pieces you have. I promise you, I will stop this disaster.'

Jake was so used to betrayal that he no longer felt surprised. He thought back, covering any clues he may have missed. The answer suddenly came to him as the abstract clues locked together.

'You can't die, can you?'

Leech smiled. 'Good guess. When the moon slams down, one of us will survive even if the rest of the world does not.'

'You have the same power as Necros?'

'You mean the powers that he had before you got rid of it? Yes, he was so much stronger because he had a bigger chunk of the pie. It was another Core Power: the power over life and death. Now it seems only I control that.' Leech's eyes twinkled.

Necros wheezed, and slumped in his chair. He barely had the strength to move. Leech continued.

'You came here expecting to battle the most dangerous villain in the world. Little did you realize that the powers the leader of the Council of Evil possessed were little more than smoke and mirrors, no more effective than any other villains'. What Necros was good at . . . was not dying. He was immortal as

long as the other Core Power we found remained intact.'

' "We found"?'

'Oh yes, I was with our good captain when we discovered this island. I was the navigator that led us here. Me and my brother, the first mate of *The Buccaneer*. The captain went mad with power and killed the crew. Kirby and I escaped, but not before we both stole a small fragment of the rock. Fragments that have kept us alive all these years. It gave the power to extend life, take life, or return from the dead. The captain became Necros as the power consumed him, and I think you know the rest of his history.'

'If it was so valuable, then why didn't he keep it secure?'

'He kept it in the bowels of an impenetrable island that few people outside the Council knew the location of. Guarded by the most terrifying villains on the planet, and a horde of other supervillain sidekicks. It was the most secure location on the planet. And you were the only one who could break it down.'

The ground shook, more terribly than before. Chunks of the chamber roof crashed down behind Jake but he didn't flinch. He was just realizing what Leech had helped him do.

'This was all a heist?'

'Exactly. Nothing more than an elaborate bank job.

The Last Stand

Everything that has taken place has done so because I wanted *everything* that Necros had. I already had a piece of his immortality. Like him and Kirby, I didn't age as fast as everybody else. Alas, the fragments we stole were weakening, we started to age. Only by periodically using my stone could I temporarily reverse the process. But the power ebbed with each use.'

'So you're dying of old age?' said Jake. 'Tough luck.'

'Why should I? Why should I wither and die while Necros keeps the lion's share of what we found?' Leech was becoming angry. 'I wanted it. In fact, I saw it as an opportunity to get everything! I don't just leech powers from others, I *collect them*. I had hoped you would retrieve his source of life and death for me, but instead you foolishly destroyed it. I could have had it, taken it far from here so Necros's powers would have been torn from him. But still, it is gone which made the next task easy. To collect his piece of the Gravity Core. Since you had done all the hard work for me, I could obtain another glorious Core Power for my collection.'

'I'm not going to let that happen,' snarled Jake. He fired a cluster of gravitons at Leech. It was a perfect shot—but nothing happened. Leech held up Necros's pendant.

'That's the problem, Jake. I have this. Even one part of the whole is enough to prevent me from coming to harm with any gravity effect you care to throw at me.

In fact, it links us together. Whatever you conjure up with it, I will have partial control too. We could fight all day, or what is left of it, but your Core Power wouldn't harm me at all.'

'Then how about this one?'

Jake fired his trusty radioactive blast at Leech. The old man wasn't expecting the attack and it burnt a hole on his shoulder. He howled, dropping behind Necros's throne for cover.

'You haven't got anything to fight back with, have you?' goaded Jake.

Leech grabbed Necros by the arm and drained what little power the villain had left.

'Now I do!' exclaimed Leech.

Jake rolled for cover as Leech hurled a fireball at him. The ground cracked as it struck and the chamber rocked as the island was bombarded again from the outside.

One of the many doors circling the chamber, each leading to a Council members' own private quarters, suddenly opened. Jake couldn't think who would be foolish enough to still be on the island as it was disintegrating. He was surprised to see Chameleon run into the chamber. The ex-hero looked around in surprise as he realized where he was.

Jake realized that he must have used the Forge equipment to trace him every time he had quantum tunnelled. Chameleon must have traced the tunnel to the Council's secret island when Jake arrived with Lorna and Orsina.

Chameleon quickly took stock of the situation—just as Leech shot at him. Chameleon jumped, changing shape in midair to a lizard and scampering up a column.

Jake tried to track him but it was too dark. Instead, he threw another radioactive blast at Leech. It exploded at the base of Necros's throne, toppling it off the ceremonial steps it was built on. The head of the Council of Evil was thrown to the floor, and Leech was left as a standing target.

Jake motioned to shoot the fiend down—but Chameleon sprang from the darkness and knocked him down. The impact caused Jake to drop the pendant wand. It skidded across the floor, out of his reach.

'Nooo!'

Like a dog after a stick, Chameleon bounded for it at the same time Leech did.

Chameleon reached it first.

He triumphantly held up the wand and activated it with a roar.

Leech was a metre away—when Necros's gnarled hand reached out and grabbed his ankle. Leech yelped as he fell, the last section of the pendant falling from his hand, sliding to Chameleon's feet.

Leech tried to boot Necros away, but the old villain's grip was like steel. 'We belong dead,' growled Necros.

Chameleon only had to point the wand at the stray piece and it leapt into place under its own gravitational forces. The assembly glowed so brightly the entire chamber was illuminated for the first time since its construction. Swirling graviton tendrils extended from the wand and snapped through the air.

'I have it!' screamed Chameleon. 'I have the ultimate power!'

Jake recognized the formation of a black hole at the tip of the wand. The air above Chameleon started to attract loose debris. The black hole was seconds away from forming.

Spacetime bent around Chameleon as he unlocked the universal power of gravity. But something wasn't right.

Chameleon's winning smirk faltered as he saw Jake was standing boldly in front of him.

In his fist, Jake clenched a piece of the pendant. He had only placed four pendants together to banish Necros's chest as he was too afraid of combining more. Now Leech's words rang in his ears—as long as he had one part, he could influence the whole. And all he wanted to do was influence it by a tiny amount.

In the skies above the Council of Evil, the descending

meteors suddenly altered trajectory as a new centre of gravity attracted them. Blazing fireballs bent impossibly towards the island.

Jake grinned ruthlessly as he stared at Chameleon, Leech, and Necros.

'All it takes, is the tiniest change,' he growled.

The ceiling above them exploded as a dozen meteors slammed into the heart of the Council chamber.

Lorna and Orsina teleported to Jake's private island chambers. It was the only place on the island they could correctly visualize. The chamber was on fire and half the wall had been demolished in a meteor strike. They could see clear across the ocean to the main island.

Lorna gasped. It truly looked like the end of the world.

The moon covered the sky, appearing blood red through the polluted atmosphere. Some of the taller lunar mountains were breaking away under the earth's gravitational pull, and lunar rocks rained down on the atmosphere, becoming meteors that hit the island.

Millions of tiny meteors bombarded the ocean— which was on fire in a circle around the island as the oil fire continued to spread.

They could only watch helplessly as countless

meteors bent towards the centre of the island and struck one after another with such ferocity that buildings toppled and entire chunks of the central island cracked away and collapsed into the flaming water like calving icebergs, kicking up a tidal wave of fiery water.

Lorna screamed Jake's name, but it was lost over the carnage.

Then the meteors stopped bending towards a single focal point and continued to descend normally. Whatever had caused them to deviate course was no longer there.

Orsina and Lorna flew over to the mainland.

Jake had downloaded the best shield he could find on Villain.net, although he doubted that it would be enough to suffer the onslaught he knew was coming. He had hoped that his patchy Duradan armour would help him, but the island's Wi-Fi had been obliterated under the celestial bombardment.

He gripped the pendant tightly as the first meteor smashed down on Chameleon. In the blink of an eye more followed, pummelling an expanding crater in the floor.

The entire chamber collapsed around him as meteors ripped through the roof. From Jake's perspective it looked as if columns of fire had descended from the heavens.

The destruction was absolute—and yet Jake, and the patch of ground he was standing on, remained intact. Nothing could reach him inside his shield. He suspected that, in ways he couldn't fathom, part of the Core Power had fused with his shield to give him the ultimate protection. After all, that's what superpowers were, descendants and spin-offs of the original Core Powers.

When the smoke cleared, there was no sign of Necros, Leech, or Chameleon—just an eight-metre deep impact crater, the walls of which bubbled with molten stone. The chamber was flattened, and Jake had an unrestricted view.

Lorna and Orsina hovered around him. Apart from the small column of floor he stood on, there was nowhere close to land.

'Are you OK?' asked Lorna with concern.

Jake nodded as his shield disbanded.

Orsina looked up at the sky. The moon was seconds away from colliding.

'Hate to be the party pooper . . . but that little fireworks show really didn't do anything to save the day.'

Jake instinctively held out his hand holding the pendant. Something stirred in the molten rubble—then the five-part pendant wand shot out—connecting perfectly to the single pendant in his hand. The bright glow turned pale blue as the Core Power was completely assembled for the first time in decades.

Lorna looked at Jake, her eyes filled with hope. 'Do you know what to do?'

Jake shook his head. 'Nope. I'm just going to click and point.'

He held the wand at the moon and unleashed the gravity force held within. He wanted to disband the black hole that had thrown the moon out of orbit, and he wanted to put the earth's satellite back where it belonged . . .

For kilometres around, the column of blue energy could be seen rising from the tiny island. It hit the moon. The entire moon glowed blue as it was gripped by gravitons that had helped shape the universe . . .

In the NORAD bunker, Bryce Campbell was so wound up staring at his screen that he accidentally farted next to the general.

One second, alarms had been squawking and collision detectors ringing—and the next . . .

Silence.

Campbell opened a tightly scrunched eye and stared at the screen.

'What's happened?' demanded the general.

'Uh . . . the moon . . . it's back to where it should be,' squeaked Campbell. 'And the meteors . . . they've stopped.' He found his voice. 'It's back to normal! Everything's back to normal!'

A massive cheer erupted inside the command centre. Even the surly general was overwhelmed by good cheer . . . until his nose twitched.

'What on earth is that smell?' he demanded.

Jake sat at the top of the mountain peak, enjoying the new day's sunshine on his face. The sky was clear blue and hordes of seagulls had appeared from nowhere to peck at the wreckage around him.

Half the Council of Evil's Island was destroyed. The other half was damaged, but serviceable. There he had found hundreds of technicians and engineers who did not have superpowers. They had been cowering away in bunkers as the villains they worked for fled around them.

A quick assessment of the remaining equipment revealed that the Villain.net bunker holding the raw powers was still intact, and the server farm would be in operation once power was restored.

Jake mused that while he had destroyed the Council of Evil, Villain.net remained.

He had defeated Necros and the Council leaders, a

goal he had set for himself but never thought he could achieve. He had brought down the Hero Foundation, although in reality that had imploded from within as Chameleon vied for power and Kirby was fired from his position at its head. Eric Kirby, the leader of the Foundation and Jake's archenemy was dead . . . even if he had turned into, not a friend, but an ally, in the end. Kirby had risked his life to defend Jake's sister. That was something Jake was trying to wrestle with.

No matter how much he thought of Beth, lying under the rubble, he couldn't cry. Maybe that's because he had seen, even in a small way, that there was a Core Power that could control life and death. Necros had had it, as did Leech.

Perhaps if Jake could find it, he could . . .

Lorna appeared next to him. She was carrying a picnic box and had been home to change. She laid the basket at Jake's feet.

'Thought you might be hungry.'

Jake smiled and gratefully ate his way through the sandwiches she had made.

Lorna looked over the devastation. 'Does this mean you'll be going back to school now?'

Jake gave her a look: *are you serious?*

Lorna smiled. 'A lot of things have changed. The Foundation's still running, trying to clear up the mess. I don't know how they're going to do it though. I think the world has finally come to accept that superpowers are very real. I can't see the Enforcers being able to cover all this up.'

'What about you?'

'Surprise, surprise, the Foundation is eager to have me back. Looks like my brother has carved himself an important position there. Pete's there too, in hospital. Something happened to him and . . . well, let's just say he won't be a threat to you any more. But never mind me. What about you? And where's what's-her-name?'

Jake smiled at the jealous tone. 'Orsina? Oh, she headed back to Forge to see what was going on there.' He saw Lorna's face cloud. 'What's the matter? What have you heard?'

Lorna poked the ground. She felt uncomfortable. 'Just rumours. Nothing substantial. But . . . but I heard Chameleon might still be alive.'

'That's impossible. I saw . . . ' Jake trailed off. *He* hadn't been hurt by the meteor storm, was it really inconceivable that Chameleon had survived? He had been channelling the power of five of the six pendants.

'They're only rumours,' Lorna reminded him. 'But the good news is that the clean-up teams found parts of Leech. He didn't survive for sure. Try and enjoy your victory. You just saved the world.' She laughed, that still didn't sound right. She looked out across the island. 'So what about this place?'

'They think they can get Villain.net up and running again.'

'So you're serious about that? What kind of villain are you? You've just overthrown the Council of Evil and saved the entire planet from annihilation. There's no hero in the Foundation who has managed to do all that!'

They both chuckled in silence before serious thoughts filled their minds. Lorna was the first to speak them.

'About your sister . . .'

'Lorn, you know me. You know why I want to see Villain.net up and running again.'

'Some things were not meant to be tampered with, Jake. Death is pretty ultimate.'

'Unless we're right about Chameleon. Somewhere out there is a Core Power that will prove you wrong. The worst thing is, we both saw it.' It was the one bolt of hope that had stopped Jake from crying with grief. He didn't see the point in telling his parents what had happened—he planned to bring Beth back before they had noticed she'd gone.

'There are lots of things out in the universe we don't understand,' said Lorna philosophically. 'That doesn't mean we should poke them with a stick.'

Jake was silent for a moment. Then he remembered something and reached into his pocket. He held out his fist.

The Last Stand

'I forgot. Happy birthday.'

He dropped a small polished black rock into her palm. 'What is it?'

'A piece of the moon that destroyed the Council chamber. I told you I'd get you something special.'

Lorna beamed at him. Jake took another sandwich and lay on his back, enjoying the sun. He closed his eyes and listened to the gulls circling for a scrap of food. The waves crashed against the cliff below, and, for the moment, he was content he had won. The thoughts of saving his sister fended off any feeling of grief.

As a villain, he realized there couldn't be a 'happy ever after'. The sheer fact there was an 'ever after' was good enough. It meant he'd lived to fight another day.

Dark Hunter had achieved his goals and done the impossible. He had to make the journey into becoming a hero, and it had been worth it. He savoured his victory.

He looked sidelong at Lorna, watching her gaze across the ocean. He thought of the old proverb: every cloud has a silver lining. In this case, the cloud had been the impending destruction of Earth. Lorna had been the lining. Jake couldn't have made it through the ordeal without her. He had a lot to be thankful for, even with the weight of the loss he had suffered.

When he woke up tomorrow, he knew with absolute certainty he would achieve the impossible again.

Andy Briggs was born in Liverpool, England. Having endured many careers, ranging from pizza delivery and running his own multimedia company to teaching IT and film-making (though not all at the same time), he eventually remembered the constant encouragement he had received at an early age about his writing. That led him to launch himself on a poor, unsuspecting Hollywood. In between having fun writing movie scripts, Andy now has far too much fun writing novels.

He lives in a secret lair somewhere in the south-east of England—attempting to work despite his three crazy cats. His claims about possessing superpowers may be somewhat exaggerated . . .

Collision Course is his fourth novel in the deviously dark 'Villain.net' series, and follows *Rise of the Heroes, Virus Attack, Crisis Point,* and *Chaos Effect* in the fiendishly clever 'Hero.com' anti-series.

Wondering about the
heroes' side of things?

Well here's a taste of

HERO.COM 4 –
CHAOS
EFFECT

Available now.
Get your hands on it!

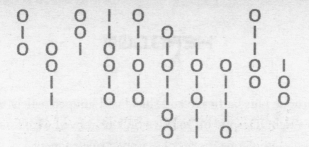

The Arrival

Lord Destructo was, in a word, unbeatable.

An expert on causing chaos, he swung the battleaxe with such devastating force that he swiped three enemies in half with a single swing, laughing evilly as he did so.

'You're goin' down!' goaded a painfully thin robed man with a crooked, pointy nose. A cone of light erupted from his palms.

Destructo was fast; in the blink of an eye he deflected the blast with a hexagonal shield. The energy ricocheted back on the thin man and he vanished in a puff of smoke.

'I am invincible!' roared Destructo. He was thoroughly enjoying himself. It had taken a long time to rise to such power, and he was determined to make the most of it. Another wave of warriors raced towards him, swords raised.

'Get him!'

'I'm gonna lob your head off, dude!'

'Nobody messes with me!' bellowed Destructo. He

dropped his battleaxe and shield and jumped agilely to his right. Despite his massive bulk he moved with fluid grace, emulating moves of seasoned free-runners.

Destructo bounced from a wall, pirouetted gracefully over his opponents' heads, then landed and dealt a flurry of martial arts blows that were almost impossible to follow.

Two of his opponents vaporized into nothing, the third was sprawled on the ground, his weapon cast aside.

'No way, man! Gimme a break!'

Destructo retrieved his battleaxe and advanced menacingly. 'Lord Destructo gives no mercy!'

'Trevor!' The voice came out of nowhere. It threw Lord Destructo off his murderous rampage. For a moment he thought his secret name had been uttered and looked around for the culprit.

'Trevor!'

It was enough of a distraction for the guy on the floor to roll to his sword and stab it into Destructo's gut. The villain recoiled, dropping his axe.

'He shoots! He scores!' hollered the swordsman jubilantly. He raised the blade for another blow.

Destructo's hands suddenly glowed bright red—a shimmering heat-ray disintegrated the swordsman. For a second, there was nothing left but a charred skeleton holding a sword, then it vanished.

'Trevor! Your dinner's going cold!'

The Arrival

Lord Destructo froze as the console game was paused. Trevor Jones irritably threw the controller down. He yanked off his headset and glared at his closed bedroom door.

'In a minute! You nearly got me killed!' he bellowed at the top of his lungs. His mum's timing was typically bad. Why was it parents always knew the moment you were having the most fun, just so they could interrupt it?

'Now, Trevor! I won't tell you again!'

'Good! I'm not hungry anyway!' he muttered under his breath.

He looked at his alter ego on the screen. It represented months of playing online and missed homework. It was a work of art, but his mum wouldn't appreciate that; apparently eating with the family was much more important. Now he would surely die if his character didn't find a safe refuge.

Trevor sighed and picked the controller up to save his game play. Out of the corner of his eye, the character seemed to move. It was a subtle thing and impossible because the game was still paused.

He squinted at the screen . . . but nothing happened. His thumb hovered over the game pad, a click away from saving the game and giving up. Then he caught the movement again in his peripheral vision.

This time the movement continued when he stared

directly at it. The graphics were distorting, each pixel shimmering. Trevor was concerned; now was not the time for the game to crash. His thumbs danced across the controller—no response.

'Don't do this to me!' He punched every button on the pad, just in case it magically restored the game. 'Great!' he spat at the screen. Resetting the console would erase the entire day's worth of play. Weighed down with reluctance, he reached for the power button—

And the screen suddenly exploded! The television itself remained intact, but the room was filled with swirling pixels as though a swarm of miniature bees had entered the room.

Trevor swatted at them as they rolled across him. It was like being inside a sandstorm. He felt sharp tingles of electricity as pixels struck him in their thousands, forcing him to his knees.

A loud CLUMP made the floor shake.

Through tear-filled eyes, Trevor watched in horror as something stepped out of the screen—something huge and muscular and alarmingly familiar.

It was Lord Destructo!